GEIR

SEALs of Steel, Book 6

Dale Mayer

GEIR: SEALS OF STEEL, BOOK 6
Dale Mayer
Valley Publishing Ltd.

ISBN-13: 978-1-773360-84-3
Print Edition

About This Book

When an eight-man unit hit a landmine, all were injured but one died. The remaining seven aim to see Mouse's death avenged.

The more Geir discovers, the more he fears the newest member of his former SEALs team wasn't who they thought.

An artist, Morning runs a B&B. She's avoided relationships but quickly decides she wouldn't mind having Geir around permanently. His protectiveness becomes much more when the nastiness of his world spills into hers...

Sign up to be notified of all Dale's releases here!
http://dalemayer.com/category/blog/

Your Free Book Awaits!

KILL OR BE KILLED

Part of an elite SEAL team, Mason takes on the dangerous jobs no one else wants to do – or can do. When he's on a mission, he's focused and dedicated. When he's not, he plays as hard as he fights.

Until he meets a woman he can't have but can't forget. Software developer, Tesla lost her brother in combat and has no intention of getting close to someone else in the military. Determined to save other US soldiers from a similar fate, she's created a program that could save lives. But other countries know about the program, and they won't stop until they get it – and get her.

Time is running out ... For her ... For him ... For them ...

DOWNLOAD a *complimentary* copy of MASON? Just tell me where to send it!

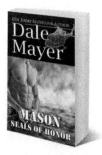

http://dalemayer.com/sealsmason/

PROLOGUE

G EIR PAVLA WATCHED the pair head back to Minx's bedroom. He was happy for his friend. Laszlo had been through so much shit and so much hurt. Minx didn't even know about his father in Norway, Geir was pretty sure. There hadn't been time. But apparently that was how life was these days. He'd watched so many of his friends come together in a combustible mode, work out their differences and, all of a sudden, be a perfect fit. He didn't expect perfection in their lives from their start. It would take time to adapt and to find a way to get along the best they could. But he knew Laszlo and Minx would make it. They were so good for each other. And Geir had no intention of interrupting their initial time together as a couple. As soon as they hit New Mexico, Geir would head to California.

He had a lot of contacts there he wasn't sure the others had. They also had a meeting in the morning. Someone in the group needed to connect with Coronado. He hoped to follow that up with a personal visit to Mason and see if they could get to the bottom of what the hell had happened with Mouse. But Geir hadn't contacted Mason to see if that could happen. At this point, Geir didn't know that he trusted anything he'd heard. None of it made any sense. But he needed to give them all an update too.

He sent out a message to Mason, telling him what happened. Even with another four hours until daylight here in Texas—meaning another six in California—Mason sent back a quick message. **Let's do the meeting when you return to New Mexico then.**

Geir agreed with that decision. The sooner they could get home, the better. He texted Mason again. **After this I'm coming down to Coronado. We're so damn close. And yet we're so far away.**

No, with every clue, you're closer, Mason texted back. **Things are happening right now, so stand strong. We'll get to the bottom of this, and it'll happen fast.**

Sure, but I need a place to stay in Coronado. I may have to call some friends.

I know somebody who runs a B&B. If you want, I can call her and get you a room. Nobody will know who you are, so you don't have to feel beholden to anyone, and you don't have to feel like you need to entertain or be entertained.

Perfect. What's her name?

Her first name is Morning. Morning Blossom.

Geir stared at the name and shook his head. **Really?**

The text came back right away. **Yeah, really. But she's a sweetheart. You'll love her.**

Geir wasn't sure. But how hard could it be to love anybody named Morning Blossom? He grinned, pocketed his phone and headed for Minx's couch. While he had the chance, he would catch a few hours of sleep because, as far as he could see, this was all coming to a head faster than ever. And he doubted he'd get Laszlo to go with him to California. But maybe. If not, well, it was time for Jager to come in out of the dark.

As he lay in the dark, Geir thought about the man he'd called best friend for so long. But Jager had taken the incident the worst. He'd been the navigator in the truck and had blamed himself. And yet, no way in hell was he responsible.

Geir sent Jager a quick message. **I know you're seeing these. I'm heading to Coronado in a couple days. Things have blown open. Road trip?**

He waited and waited, and, when he thought, *No way in hell would Jager break his silence*, Geir got a message. He read it and grinned.

I'll be there.

CHAPTER 1

G EIR STEPPED OUT of the airport and stopped. It had been several years since he'd been in California. Although there were some ugly memories, there were a lot of good ones. The nostalgia truck hit him hard. He gave himself all of thirty seconds to wallow, and then he straightened his back and headed for the rental agency. The truck was something familiar, fun and reminiscent of their old life, and he never knew when he might need to haul something.

Mason had booked Geir at a bed-and-breakfast run by Morning Blossom. She even had a website for Morning Blossom's Bed-&-Breakfast. He wondered how somebody not only was given a name like that but had liked the name enough to use it as her business name for her B&B. He shook his head. Geir had some work to figure out, some information to define. They were so damn close to getting to the bottom of their land mine mystery that he didn't want to waste any time thinking about strange business names.

If he could finish up here in California in a couple days, then get back to New Mexico, he'd be happy. The rest of the unit were hunting down information. Geir could just envision the entire team leaning over laptops and on their phones. Last he'd heard before he had boarded the plane to leave Santa Fe was that the Afghanistan arms dealer had contacted Erick. Seems that, approximately two years ago—

same timing as their land mine accident—the local rebel leader had had somebody working for him who'd been inciting change within his ranks. The leader had thought he had taken measures to derail any upstarts back then. However, with the latest happenings in Kabul—when Erick, Cade and Talon were there about a month ago—in a permanent effort to remove that threat, the rebel leader had cleaned house … completely this time.

Geir tried to understand what possible connection this asshole could have to his unit's accident over there. At this point, he could only figure the rebel leader's henchman had been paid to do a freelance job by some third-party. Nothing else made sense. And it was far too late to question him.

Geir changed lanes yet again. Another thing he'd forgotten about San Diego was the damn traffic.

It took twenty minutes longer than planned, but eventually he pulled up to a large multilevel yellow Victorian-looking clapboard house.

He parked the truck out on the road and walked up to the front door with its big Welcome, Come In sign. He shrugged, opened the door and stepped inside. Immediately a light fresh scent filled his nostrils, one he hadn't smelled in a long time. He tilted his head to the side, hearing a voice call from the back, "I'll be right there."

He lifted his nose appreciatively to fresh-baked bread.

He dropped his bag quietly and followed the voice. There, in a large country-style kitchen, with pine cupboards and a massive butcher-block island, was a woman, her hair up in a messy bun, tendrils of reddish auburn hair dancing around her temples, working with a large bowl of foamy liquid.

He stopped and spoke to her. "Since you're busy, I hope

you don't mind that I came to find you." His tone was quiet, almost apologetic.

She glanced up and beamed.

He was struck by the openness in her smile. He was a complete stranger who'd walked into her house. Didn't she know better? Didn't she know the world was full of darkness and evil? Filled with men who would do horrible things, even if they were family or friends?

"Delighted to meet you." Her voice was light, soft. "You must be Geir."

He frowned. "I must? Why?"

"Because you're exactly as Mason described you."

At that, his eyebrows rose. "Not sure Mason knows that much about me."

"Oh, he didn't tell me that you had brown hair and were six feet tall." She laughed. "He said that I'd know you by the stillness in your stance, the look in your eyes, the hardness to your jaw and that, inside, you were a teddy bear."

He couldn't hold back the snort. His grin widened. "Did he also warn you about leaving your door unlocked for anybody to walk in?"

She chuckled. "Mason and many others have told me that repeatedly. I have security out there. I guess it'll only help after the fact and not do a damn bit of good beforehand." She nodded at the island cluttered with her current project. "And thank you for coming in. I wasn't looking forward to cleaning off my hands and then getting back to work. This stuff is so messy."

"*Stuff?*"

She chuckled. "This is a ripe sourdough starter I'm adding to, but I wanted to give it a good mix. Instead, I dropped my spoon in, so I had to fish it out." She held up a spoon completely covered in some gloopy mess. She walked to the sink, washed her hands and the spoon. "I'll put on a fresh pot of coffee. Would you like a cup?"

"Yes, thank you. And do I smell fresh bread baking?"

She tossed him a saucy look. "Fresh bread *and* homemade cinnamon buns. See? You have perfect timing."

He heard the front door open again. Somewhere in the house chimes rang.

She gave a nod of satisfaction. "Both of you have great timing."

"How could you possibly know who the other person is?"

She nodded behind him, and he turned toward a small TV. Onscreen was somebody Geir hadn't seen in two years. His face lit up. "Jager." He spun on his heels and headed out to the front hall.

The two men wrapped their arms around each other in a hard, long hug. Both emotional, Geir stepped back. "Well, I'm glad nobody else saw that."

Jager nodded, his voice husky as he said, "True enough."

Of course Geir realized Morning Blossom would have seen it via her security setup, but it appeared to be something she wouldn't have a problem with. He looked at Jager. "It's been a long time."

"Not only a long time but a long distance. I almost died," Jager said bluntly.

Geir nodded. "Me too. After that blast, the first couple weeks were just a nightmare of surgeries and drugs and hospital beds and operating rooms. It took me weeks to even get an idea of where I was. Only to wake and find I was missing parts of me."

Jager nodded. "I think I have more pins in my body now

than it's possible to have and still be alive."

"Modern medicine." Geir nodded. "Thank God."

"I didn't think so for a long time though." Jager's voice dropped painfully. "I begged for them to let me go. Told them that I refused to have any more surgery. Made sure they posted a Do Not Resuscitate order if I coded one more time."

Geir winced.

"I didn't have to do that," Jager said quietly. "Yet, at that time, it was the only way I could handle things."

"But, if you think less of yourself for having hit that stage, don't," Geir said. "Most of us got thrown into the shit pile and back out again. Some of us survived, and we're okay. Some of us survived, and we're less than okay. But, I got to tell you, the others in the group, they're doing pretty damn decent."

"What's this I hear about women?"

"Glad you said *women*, plural. Maybe we had a little bit too much to do with Mason's bloody matchmaking group. So far, all the others, all five of them, have picked up partners who are incredible," Geir said. "And honestly, a part of me is feeling sad for myself. I'm not jealous of them— maybe envious—but I wouldn't want to take away from their joy. Every one of us had hit the shit soup. We've all eaten from that same shit sandwich, so it's nice if somebody gets a chance to pull out of it."

"I gather your recovery was far from ideal?"

Geir snorted. "You might have extra pins, but I'm missing more organs than I thought one could live without."

Jager nodded. "You took more of a soft-tissue blast then, I presume?"

Geir shrugged. "I did. Of course that's in addition to the

loss of my right hand and my right lower leg, but that's almost a *So what?* in our group."

Just then a voice behind them said, "If you guys want to come to the kitchen, there's fresh coffee." Morning stepped through the doorway. "Glad you two have finally reconnected." She motioned with her arm. "Coffee is this way."

Geir looked at his bag. "I need to take this to my room first."

Jager had yet to put his down.

She took one look at the two of them, eyed their bags and gave a quick nod. "If you have weapons in there, just know you aren't allowed to brandish them in my house."

Jager tilted his head and smiled. "And what if we have a just need?"

Her eyes widened. "Well, it hasn't happened in any of my years. Yet, I suppose, if a situation arose where gunfire was required, then I'd have to say, *Thank you*, in advance."

Geir chuckled. "You're thanking us for having weapons you don't want us to have in the house?"

"Only in the hypothetical circumstance that they might be necessary down the road," she said cheerfully. She stepped behind the small front counter, flipping open to a new page on the guest book. "Sign here. Payments have already been processed."

"What?" Geir asked. "By whom?"

She looked at him with a smile. "Mason. For both of you. And maybe that's because I require an advance payment."

Geir nodded. "He would do something like that."

Morning waited until both men signed the book, then picked up two keys, handed them over and held up her big ring of keys. "I have masters for both your rooms." She came from around the counter. "Follow me."

MORNING WALKED UP the stairs to the second floor. Mason had specifically asked for one bedroom in the front and one bedroom in the back but connected. She wasn't too sure of the status of the two men's relationship, but she had been too moved by their greeting to judge. They obviously shared a deep and strong bond, and that was priceless. She stopped at the first bedroom, opened the door and stepped in.

She was proud of her rooms here. She had three stories, four rooms on each level, and her own was the alcove in the back of the third floor. Sometimes she was full; sometimes she wasn't. Running a bed-and-breakfast had both benefits and disadvantages. But, so far, the benefits had outweighed all the disadvantages.

"Here you go. This is one of the two rooms. The other one is connected by this door." She walked to the interior door and opened it. "So, you can either close and lock this, from both sides, or you can sit here and have midnight supersecret meetings," she joked, watching as the two men looked around the spacious room with the large king-size bed and a small balcony off the front. "I'm not sure which one of you wants this one. Let's go through to the second one." She walked through the connecting doorway. "This is the matching room. These two make up half of the second story, with another pair on the other side of this floor. So you'll have a front view and a back view."

"Fire escape?" Jager asked.

She glanced at him in surprise. "There isn't one. There is a back staircase, and you can access it from this bedroom."

She walked out into the hall and motioned to the staircase that led down the back way. "There are two entrances and exits. The balcony is also one floor off the ground, if necessary as an emergency exit. I'm sure you could get out of there fairly safely."

Both men nodded but didn't say a word.

She wasn't sure what to make of them. It was obvious they were powerfully capable men, as every step they took had that sense of determination behind it, driving them forward. They also held themselves aloof, as if they weren't sure of their welcome in the world. Or as if they'd separated themselves for some reason.

She smiled at them. "And now that you are here, you decide which room you want. I don't need to know because I've given you keys. One of you has one for this room. The other has the other. Obviously, if you need to change, go ahead and change. I'll go check on the cinnamon buns." She gave them another smile, slipped into the hall and went down the back stairwell. It would take her just outside the kitchen, with a back door exit, mudroom, storage and pantry there.

She walked into the kitchen, hearing the timer going off on the stove. She picked up her pace, grabbed her oven mitts, opened the oven door and pulled out a tray of beautifully golden cinnamon buns, the sugar just bubbling over the top. She smiled and set them on the big butcher-block island. With the oven open, she rearranged the bread baking inside and closed it up, setting the timer for another twenty minutes.

The bread was looking good, but in no way was it done yet. At the island, she put the cinnamon buns on a rack to cool and poured herself a cup of coffee. The sourdough starter was ready to be put away, which she did, then she considered what was next on her list.

The men hadn't arrived in time for breakfast, but she certainly didn't have a problem offering them coffee or iced tea. It was only eleven in the morning. She'd had two groups leave this morning already, so she still had linens to change and laundry to do.

Just as she thought maybe she'd get that done before the men came downstairs, she could hear them arriving already.

As they walked in, Geir's face lit up. "Cinnamon buns. They look delicious."

"Glad you think so." She put out two mugs and poured them coffee. "Help yourself."

She grabbed two plates and handed them over with a set of tongs. Both men took two cinnamon buns each. She grinned. "I knew when Mason called to reserve your rooms that you would be big eaters."

They slid her a sideways look, but neither could talk because their mouths were full.

She shrugged. "Now that you've checked in, I'll give you the basic rules. We shut down the house at eleven p.m., so please be back by then. Breakfast will be served between seven and ten. Checkout is at eleven. Mason has you booked for three days and three nights, counting today, Tuesday, through Thursday night until check out time on Friday morning. If you need to change that, just let me know." She gave them a brighter smile. "I have to switch out laundry from the two groups that just left this morning."

"Do you have more coming in today?"

"I have a party coming in at four this afternoon. They'll only be staying overnight and then heading out again."

"That's interesting. They stay here and not at a hotel

close to the airport?"

She nodded. "I think they're more comfortable in a house environment."

"Do you provide dinners?"

She turned to them at that. "Not as part of the package, but I certainly will provide dinner if you can give me a time you'll be here and some general idea of what you'd enjoy eating."

The two men exchanged glances, then shrugged. Geir said, "Our schedule is a bit up in the air."

"Then we'll touch base on that concept a little later. I'm planning on making shepherd's pie for dinner, and, if there's any thought that you two might join me, I'll make a bigger one. You can always warm up a plate when you come in."

Both men brightened. "That would suit us just fine," Geir said. "Thank you."

She nodded and slipped from the kitchen.

There was something compelling about Geir. A sense of deep waters inside. She wanted to sit down and study him. He was a fascinating person to her. Jager was a little darker personality wise than she was used to, a little quieter, a little more stoic. Almost everyone who came to her bed-and-breakfast were friendly, family-oriented, fun-loving types. These men were more isolated—detached. For that reason, she was grateful they had each other. Life would be damn lonely if they didn't have that.

Mason hadn't given her any of their background information, and she hadn't asked. Right now, questions were bubbling up to the surface. She knew it wasn't part of her job, and, as part of the respect the patrons held for her, she didn't ask too many questions.

She headed to the two bedrooms that had emptied and

quickly changed out the linens. A washer and dryer were on each of the floors, which made her life a little easier. She started the laundry, remade the beds, grabbed the vacuum, cleaned up the rooms and then headed to the bathrooms for each. Thankfully both were reasonably clean, just needing a good wipe down.

When she was done, she returned to the kitchen to check if the men needed more coffee. The room was empty, their cups and plates washed and set on the draining rack to dry. She looked at the cinnamon bun pan. They had eaten the two each, and that was it.

She hadn't heard them go upstairs, yet hadn't heard them leave. They'd been incredibly silent. She frowned, wondering if that was an issue. It shouldn't be. But she was used to friendlier, transparent guests. She shrugged and headed to her office. There was always paperwork to be done. She tried to work an eight-hour day, but that never really happened. Did any person who owned their own business get to have that luxury?

She ran this place herself, and it was only when she had multiple people coming in for breakfast all at the same time that she got a little flustered. Any other time, well, it was her home, and she just opened the doors to let the world in. Mason had chastised her more than a couple times about being too trusting. She had told him how most of her business was word of mouth. That helped a lot to ensure she had business but also that she and her guests were relatively safe, since Morning dealt with reputable people. She had a website, but she didn't put any money into ads. So far she hadn't needed to.

As soon as she got through her paperwork, she straightened her back, already aching from the hard chair. She glared down at the old thing. "Definitely past time to replace you," she muttered.

The trouble was, as much as she did okay, she didn't spend money on extras because something in the plumbing would always go awry, and she needed that little bit of saved-up money to handle it. She shrugged irritably and walked back into the kitchen. She could have brought her laptop and done some of her paperwork out here. It didn't matter now that she was done with it for today.

She did a quick check, found the house was empty and that the men were gone. She looked out the living room window. No vehicles were parked at her curb. She'd seen the truck pull up that Geir had arrived in but had no idea what Jager had driven. And it was none of her business, she had to remind herself.

What she did have was a couple hours of free time. She headed to her bedroom, quickly changed into a clean painting smock and walked into her adjoining studio. One of the reasons she had opened her home as a B&B was because it gave her the chance to continue with her main passion, her painting. She had a gallery opening coming up in six months, and she didn't have anywhere near enough paintings for it. And the ones she did have, she didn't like.

She should probably show them to the gallery owner and see if they were even a possibility. The owner was doing this as a favor for a mutual friend, and she kind of hated that. She wanted to be offered a show on her own merit, but her friend had been very clear, telling Morning not to be too stupid or too proud to accept the gift horse offered. And that was right, but, at the same time, it was wrong.

She stared at the painting on the easel in front of her and frowned. "You look like shit," she said in disgust. Instead of picking up her brush, she threw herself on the futon she kept here and stared up at the canvases around her. They were all touristy-looking scenes. They were all pretty, but she didn't want to do *pretty*. She wanted drama. She wanted the painting to tell her something, to have the viewer look at it and get sucked in for the ride. These didn't do that. They were gift-shop paintings. And that was *so* not where her heart was. The trouble was, she was running out of time.

Her phone rang. She pulled her cell from her pocket and groaned. Of course. It was the gallery owner. With a wince she straightened. "Hi, Leon. How are you?"

"Still waiting to see samples of what you're bringing in for the show."

"Right. I have a busy day today." She thought about that white lie, not happy with herself. "Today is Tuesday. ... How about Friday?"

"Friday, it is. Make sure you've got something good. I'm looking forward to seeing this. You come highly recommended." And he hung up.

She glared at her phone and then tossed it on the futon. "No pressure though, right?"

The trouble was, she had put the pressure on herself. She could take these paintings to him, but she knew he wouldn't like them. Hell, *she* didn't even like them. What she needed was something that showed who and what she was on the inside, and that wasn't necessarily anything she could do. Not yet. Too risky. She wasn't ready.

She sat for a long moment, hearing her father. He was a voice in the back of her mind. *Really? You'll give up so easily?*

She shuddered. She'd spent a lifetime being a people-pleaser personality. Somewhere in her early or late teens, she realized she was a sunny kind of person. She sat up straight as she stared at the painting she'd already shot down. She got up, took it off the easel, set it on the floor against the wall. "Okay, so these are all right. But they don't show my true personality. They don't show the sunshine within. The light, that sparkle I feel attuned to," she muttered.

She put a clean canvas on the stand and pulled out the yellow tube of paint. She stared at it for a long moment and then frowned. "Okay, so maybe not quite so yellow."

She closed her eyes. "I need to trust I have what it takes to do this. The fear is crippling me. Show me the way. I trust in me. I trust in myself. Please help me find what I need to do right now."

She opened up two tubes of paint, a winter white and a pale lemon, then turned back to the canvas.

CHAPTER 2

"HELLO? ANYONE HERE?"

Morning jolted with a start. She froze as she stared at the canvas, her gaze narrow. "Sorry. I'm coming," she yelled.

"No problem. Just wondered if you were here."

Dimly, in the back of her mind, she recognized the voice of one of her new guests. Just then Geir popped his face around the doorway. She stared at him in surprise. "Guests aren't allowed in here."

He nodded, but, instead of backing up, he stepped into the room. He looked at all the paintings she had set aside, potentially for the gallery, and he didn't look quickly. Instead, he picked up each one, studied it, put it down, picked up another one.

She could feel herself not breathing, waiting for his comment, whether it was disparaging or complimentary. But he didn't say a word. He studied them all, put them back, turned to look around, saw the futon, then came up behind her. She froze. She hated for anybody to see her paintings in progress. She knew it came from her well of self-doubt, worrying how each wasn't a masterpiece. She could see what she wanted in her mind's eye, but she hadn't been able to get her fingers to match that same image on a canvas. *Yet.*

She stepped back until she stood beside him and turned

her gaze to the canvas on the easel. She frowned. What the hell? Had she done that? Just then her grandfather clock chimed downstairs, and she realized it was four o'clock. She gasped. "It can't be that late already."

Geir slid her a glance. "Well, it is."

Horrified, she looked at him, glanced back at the painting but couldn't comprehend what she saw. She walked to the sink, cleaned her brushes and washed her hands.

When her hands were paint-free, she pulled off her smock and returned to take another look at the painting. It wasn't just good. It was stunning. She knew it wasn't finished, but, for the first time, she knew what was supposed to go next. It was an early morning sunrise, peeking through the clouds, adding light and lightness to a cherry blossom tree opening its buds. It was mostly done. She had a few more highlights to add. Several more hours probably because she always slowed down at this stage. But it was everything she could have hoped it to be.

At the same time she wondered if she was just caught up in the euphoria of a new project and not seeing it clearly. Then she turned to look at her *nice* paintings and knew there was no comparison. This wasn't so much *nice* as it was *demanding*. It sucked you in and held you there.

And still Geir hadn't said anything. He stood silently at her side, staring at the painting.

She walked to the door. "I'd like you to come out of there now please."

He glanced at her, his gaze piercing as he said, "If you can paint like this"—he motioned to the canvas on the easel—"why do you paint like that?" He pointed to the pictures on the floor.

She stopped and looked at him. "What do you mean?"

"The level, the intensity, it's tenfold in this painting. This one draws you in. I want to be there on that cherry blossom branch, watching the sunrise. It's full of possibilities. It's full of hope. Those others are flatter, still pretty, but this ..." He returned his gaze to the canvas in front of him. "It's stunning."

Inside she felt some of the walls she'd built over her art dissolve. Some of her own insecurities came crumbling down. "Thank you," she said quietly. "I have to come up with some paintings to take to a gallery owner on Friday. And I was unhappy with what I'd already done. I was looking for something that defined me, who I am. And I honestly don't remember very much about the last few hours. I got so caught up in the painting."

He walked toward her. "So that painting is going in a gallery. It'll be for sale?"

She nodded. "Hopefully. If he likes it."

"If he doesn't like it, I would like to buy it."

She turned and looked at him. He nodded. "I'm serious. It's really beautiful."

Her heart bursting with happiness, she practically danced her way downstairs into the kitchen.

As Geir followed her, he said, "Tell me about the gallery showing."

She shrugged as she pulled out the preparations for her shepherd's pie, knowing she had to work fast. While she talked, she got the meat cooking, chopped up vegetables and put on the potatoes. "Not a whole lot to tell. A friend of a friend got me the invitation, and I was feeling uncomfortable, thinking I didn't earn it on my own."

"Some of the best breaks in the business world come from word of mouth," he said neutrally. "You can't let that stop you from taking advantage of it."

She shrugged. "I've always been self-conscious about my art. I felt like I couldn't quite connect to that part of my soul that needed to express what was in my head and in my heart. But with that painting, the most recent one, I feel like maybe I finally made a tentative step in that direction."

"It shows incredible promise." He looked around. "Any chance of a cup of coffee?"

She nodded. "Absolutely." She put on a pot and returned to chopping the vegetables.

Twenty minutes later, she had the meat browned, all the vegetables collected, and a thick gravy just waiting on the potatoes. He saw what she was about to do and said, "Let me drain those."

He took the pot off the stove and drained out the moisture, took off the lid, and, while she poured in cream, butter and spices, he mashed the potatoes into a nice thick topping for the vegetables and meat. It took another ten minutes to get it all assembled into the pan and into the oven.

She exhaled and smiled. "Phew! That's done." She turned the temperature up on the oven. "Dinner will be in an hour."

"Absolutely," he said with a smile.

"How did your afternoon go?" she asked.

"Actually I wanted to ask if Jager was here. I haven't seen him since this morning."

"I haven't seen him either." She turned and looked at Geir. "Is that a problem?"

"I don't know," he admitted. "I headed off to meet someone, but he didn't show. Now I can't connect with Jager." Clearly Geir was frustrated. "So far it feels like today has been a complete waste. I was hoping Jager had better luck."

"I'm not sure I can do anything to help you in your reason for being here, but I haven't seen Jager since you left. Then again, I didn't hear you leave, so ..." She held out her hands. "Did you check his room?"

Geir nodded. "He's not there."

"Vehicle?"

"Not there."

"Did you call him?"

"He hasn't answered his phone."

She leaned her hands on the edge of the counter and stared at Geir. "Is this serious? Do we need to call the police?"

He shook his head. "It wouldn't be the police I'd call because what we're doing here is private, for lack of a better word. I need to give Jager time to get back to me." Then his phone rang. He smiled and held it up. "Jager. Hey, where are you?" Instantly he froze. "I'm on my way." He walked out of the kitchen, calling over his shoulder, "You may have to hold plates for us."

She trailed behind him. "Why? What happened?"

"Jager just called. He was tracking somebody we know."

"And?"

Geir turned to look at her. "He found a body."

GEIR HOPPED INTO his truck, pulled out into the traffic and headed downtown. His phone rang again. He clipped it on the dashboard and hit Talk. "Jager, I'm on my way."

"Good. So are the cops." His voice was dry. "I'm not in a very good position here."

"Do you know who it is?"

"No, but, according to somebody I just talked to, he was a friend of Poppy's."

Geir's back stiffened. "How good a friend?"

"That's the thing, isn't it? Apparently Poppy is well-known for his friends."

"And that would include Mouse, I presume?"

"I asked him about Mouse, and he said he'd seen him around. But not for a few years."

"Well, he's been dead for two. He was in our unit for a third so how many does a *few* years mean?"

"He disappeared before he could answer anything else," Jager said. "I have a good idea where he went though. It might be worth our while to give him a good shakedown, see what else he might have for information."

"Was he close to the body?"

"Yes, but he took one look, then tried to bolt. I grabbed him, told him that I didn't have anything to do with it." He shrugged. "That body has been here for a while."

"And of course he didn't call for help?"

"Pretty sure he figured there was no point in trying to help because there was no help to be given."

"According to the GPS, I'll be there in seven minutes."

"I'm in the back alley, so park on the main street."

"Will do." He ended the call, returning his attention to the traffic. Did one ever get used to heavy traffic? He followed the traffic until he came to the end of the GPS line. Seeing where the alley was, he waited for somebody to pull out from the main street, then nipped in and took a spot. Not knowing how long he would be here, but realizing there would be loads of cops, he put change into the meter, then walked around to the alley. "Jager?"

"Yep, keep coming this way."

"Cops here?"

"Not yet."

Geir shook his head. "Cop response time is different here, I presume?"

"Seems like it. It's been at least thirty minutes."

Almost before he got the words out, the sounds of a siren filled the air.

"Why the sirens now?"

The black-and-white pulled into the alley and stopped at the entrance. Geir stood beside Jager and waited. The cops approached. "Are you the ones who called us?"

Jager stepped forward. "I did." He pointed to a heap of clothing beside a Dumpster bin. "That's where I found the body."

"Did you check if he was dead?"

"I did. I'd say he's been dead at least a couple hours."

"Why would you say that?"

"Because rigor has set in."

The cop sent him a hard glance. "Are you a doctor?"

Jager shook his head and just stayed quiet.

Geir understood. Jager had been the best medic of all of them in the unit. He had patched them up time and time again. And, if Jager said it was this many hours, then Geir believed him. But the cops would just get suspicious. And no one in the unit wanted to rehash who they were and how they came by their knowledge. Still, it was something that would likely have to be clarified at some point.

Geir stood silently while the cops talked to Jager about what he'd seen and heard.

The lead cop asked, "Do you know who it was you spoke to?"

Jager shook his head. "The guy disappeared around the corner." He shrugged. "I'm pretty sure it was a homeless guy."

"In this area, most likely." The cop turned his attention to Geir. "And you?"

"I came down because he told me what he'd found."

"Curious?"

"Supporting a friend," he clipped out.

The cop nodded. "We need your contact information. Then you better clear out. We'll have the coroner here in no time."

Both willingly handed over their details and cell phone numbers. And, when they were free to go, they walked down the street and stood beside Geir's truck. Jager's Jeep Wrangler was parked around the corner.

Geir looked at his buddy. "I don't think we should leave until we track down the guy you talked to. Look for a few more answers."

"As long as we're not seen," Jager warned. "We know perfectly well the cops will look at us suspiciously if we get into their investigation."

Geir nodded. "But chances of coming back here tomorrow and finding this homeless guy are not good."

Jager agreed. "Lead the way."

Together they sauntered down the block, turned right, went up a block to what looked like an old storefront with the windows busted out. Jager stepped to the door and pushed it open. Inside they stilled and listened. The sound of scurrying footsteps could be heard off in the far right corner. Moving quietly, they slid up the stairs and confronted two people sitting in the corner, a jug of booze between them. One man yelped, ready to run.

Jager held up his hands. "I'm not here to hurt you."

The other guy froze and picked up his booze bottle, taking a big slug. "I don't know nothing," he said.

The first man shook his head. "And I told you all I did know."

"We're looking for Poppy," Geir said. "Where can we find him?"

The guy shook his head. "You don't want to find Poppy."

"Why is that?"

"Poppy doesn't like cops."

"We're not cops," Geir said.

"You look close enough to it, and you won't fool Poppy."

Geir knew that was probably true. "We're trying to find information about a friend. His nickname is Mouse," he said, a part of him knowing perfectly well the Mouse they were after had died in the accident that had left Jager and him and the others badly injured. But, on the off chance there were *two* men called Mouse, Geir wanted to make sure they covered all the bases.

"Haven't seen him in years," the man said, then belched aloud, an offending odor wafting Geir's way.

"Who could we ask for more information?"

The guy shook his head.

Jager pulled out his wallet, and, all of a sudden, the man smiled. "Well now, if you got a little bit of money there, I might tell you something."

The second man nodded his head. "We got information."

"Yeah, really? What kind of information? We'll pay you, depending on how valuable it is," Jager said, his voice hard.

"Poppy and Mouse. What can you tell us?"

The words spilled out. "Haven't seen Mouse in a couple years—maybe three or four," one man said. "Poppy is around. At least I haven't heard anything different. I avoid being anywhere he is, so I haven't seen him in a long while."

"Mouse is that tall skinny guy, right?" the second man asked.

Geir nodded. "Yes, that's him. Would have been about twenty-five, twenty-six some four years ago."

"He was Poppy's boy."

"I know. That's why we're trying to find Poppy."

"You don't look like you prefer boys," the second man said.

"We don't," Jager said. "But we do want to find Mouse."

"Is he a friend of yours?" the second man asked, his eyes blurry, his face red.

Geir nodded. "A very dear friend."

Maybe he shouldn't have said it that way because both of the winos looked at him suspiciously. He raised both palms. "No, we don't want him for that reason."

Both men shrugged. "Mouse and Poppy have been together a long time."

"Since Mouse took off, who does Poppy hang around with?"

"Others," the second man said. "Lots of others."

"And, when he was with Mouse, were they together-together?"

The second man nodded. "Seemed like it. Like I said, I haven't seen Poppy in a while. He went back to his old ways."

"What were the old ways?"

The second man froze, looked at the other guy.

The other guy picked up the story. "He likes lots of young boys. When he was with Mouse, he seemed to be stable. But, after Mouse left, he went back to little boys."

"And the cops never caught him?"

"No, he's looking for another Mouse. Somebody he can groom for the long term."

"So, another boy looking for a father figure, love and attention, plus three square meals a day," Jager said, his tone harder than before.

Both men nodded. "Exactly," the second man said.

"So you need to help us find Poppy, so we can help these boys."

The second man picked up the jug and took a big slug. "Check out the school."

"Which one?"

"Around the corner," he said. "Sometimes Poppy brings them there."

Geir looked around at the deserted building, the drafty windows, and thought about a man bringing a young boy desperate for attention to a place like this. "For booze, drugs or sex?"

"All of them. Depends what the kids need."

With a grim nod, Jager asked, "Do you know anything about Mouse?"

"He was tight with Poppy for a long time. And then something happened. And Mouse left."

"Do you know for sure he left? Any chance Poppy might have taken him out?"

Both men shook their heads. "Poppy doesn't kill," the first man said. "He's the kind that'll bawl and beg before he'll kill anyone."

"So is that why he went off the wall after Mouse left? Grief? Broken up over the breakup? Had to find a replacement?"

The men nodded again.

"Any idea who killed the guy outside?"

Both men shared a glance and a shrug. "No," said one of them.

"Was he a friend of Poppy's?"

"No, but it's not hard to imagine another man or a family member getting upset at somebody Poppy may have touched," the other man said.

"Why haven't they caught him?"

"Because he's slimy and ugly on the inside, but you don't see that on the outside," the first man said.

Geir stiffened. "And when you say, *around the school*, you don't mean hanging around the playground, looking to lure a young boy. What you mean is working *in* the school, don't you?"

The second man nodded. "Yeah, he works there. You can't miss him. He's the one the kids all love."

"Hence the name Poppy?" Geir surmised.

"And what's Poppy's real name?" Jager asked.

Both men shrugged. "I think you've had enough information for whatever money you're passing our way," the first man said.

Geir and Jager exchanged looks.

"They have been helpful," Jager said in a low tone. He pulled forty bucks out of his wallet and stepped forward, handing each of the men a twenty.

Instantly the money disappeared, and both smiled up at him. "Thanks very much. If you ever need any more information, you know where to find us."

"Well, considering there's a dead man outside, you might want to change your location," Geir said. "Somebody else might not pay you with money in return for information. They might decide to pay you by shutting you up."

The men's gazes turned to beady-eyed ferret-looking things. "We'll be moving real fast," the second man said, finally understanding.

"What killed him?" the first one asked.

"Don't know. His head was bashed in."

"Shit. I really liked this place. We'll have to leave it for at least a month now."

"Well, that's how long we had to leave it last time," the first man agreed.

At that, Geir asked, "How often have Poppy's friends been killed?"

The men glanced at him. The first man said, "He goes through a lot of friends." After that he shut up, wouldn't say anymore.

Back downstairs and out on the street, Geir had to think about that. "So, if it's not Poppy killing people, who is it?"

"And are any of them connected or is it just a random issue—or is Poppy hiring people to do his dirty work?"

"We're just starting this investigation, so it's too early to tell."

Jager checked his watch. "I suggest we go talk to the school."

"Well, Minx's friend Agnes led us to a JoJo Henderson aka Poppy in the halfway house in Texas, but that went cold once he moved on. And we find no paper trail of a JoJo Henderson here in San Diego. We still have to find out what name Poppy is using here," Geir said, falling into step beside his buddy. "But I guess working at a school would be a great place to find your next victim, wouldn't it?"

"And potentially a lot of very angry parents, if you picked the wrong student."

Geir nodded. "Sounds like he's trying to replace Mouse though. Particularly if he managed to get Mouse into the navy. Poppy could be very lonely."

"That brings up another point. We never did ask if there was any physical reason Mouse couldn't join the navy. Maybe we need to follow up with Minx some more."

"Would she know? He apparently was physically scarred from all these years of bodily trauma, but it's also quite possible he wouldn't pass the shrink exam."

"I'm surprised any of us passed some of those tests," Jager said quietly.

"Exactly."

CHAPTER 3

THE SHEPHERD'S PIE sat on the island, but nobody was here to eat it. Her four o'clock group had already called to tell her that they were running late. Morning studied the golden bubbly top and wondered about Geir and Jager. They'd given her their phone numbers, but she didn't want to text either to let them know dinner was ready. Geir had been here when she'd put it into the oven, and he knew when dinner was planned for.

Shrugging, she got a plate and served herself a small portion. She added a green salad on the side, sat at her kitchen counter and ate alone.

It wasn't often that her house was empty. And, while it was, she should be taking advantage of it. She looked around the kitchen, wishing she'd had the money to redo various parts of the residence. It was old, and she had had several developers already on her case, asking her to sell to them so they could drop her house and put up some big fancy million-dollar home.

If she had had anything else to do with her life, she might consider it. But this was her anchor. This was her safe place. But she wasn't the sole owner. It was her and her father. After he had moved to Europe to do research with his new girlfriend, Morning had bought half of it. She'd needed him as a cosigner at the time.

After a few years he wanted to sell his remaining half and get the rest of his money out of his asset. She didn't want to sell, but no way could she buy him out. Particularly with the current real estate prices. Her father had contacted her about the idea several times, but she'd always pushed back, saying she wasn't ready. Anytime something went wrong, he should be paying half the maintenance costs, but he wasn't— because she was the one *making money off it and not sharing the profit.*

But she wasn't making tons. She made enough to live on, but that was about it. It certainly wouldn't ever be enough to buy out her father. The decision was looming, ... but it made her queasy to think about it.

She cleaned up her dishes, made herself a cup of tea and then went to her third-floor studio, adjoining her bedroom and en suite bath, her own private area. She hadn't let herself look at the painting since Geir had been here.

She was still walking on cloud nine from his praise, but, at the same time, she knew the harshest judge of her work was herself. And what she needed was to make sure it was as good as she had first thought it was. And the second glimpse might tell her. Unfortunately the studio didn't have a ton of light at this hour of the day.

She flicked on all the lights before walking to stand in front of the painting. She gasped for joy. It was ... special. So much more of what she wanted to present to the world.

She threw on her smock again, and, with a fine paintbrush, quickly touched up the blossoms, picking up a brighter pink, adding a touch of yellow, until the entire canvas glowed.

Then her sense of self glowed too. She was absolutely overjoyed with this piece.

Finally she was satisfied and walked to the sink to wash her brushes again. She checked the clock and realized another two hours had passed.

She didn't have a clue where the men were. Maybe they were downstairs already, and she'd missed them.

This painting had just completely sucked her into the process. That was a good thing. With a happy sigh, she turned for one last look at the canvas, feeling pride in this piece of work for the first time in a long time. "Maybe I can make that Friday appointment after all."

After closing her studio, she walked back downstairs and around to her office. She logged off her computer, checked if anybody was around and found nobody.

"Works for me." She made herself a second cup of tea and headed out on the back porch to the huge lounger sitting out there. She stretched out and just relaxed. Today was a good day. She'd started on a path with her painting that was something she would be proud to show somebody else.

Just then her phone rang. She pulled it out. Nancy calling. Hitting Talk, Morning said, "What's up?"

"Well, I've been trying to call you off and on all day," her friend said. "Who are the two hunks living at your place? And how come you didn't share?" her friend complained.

"Geir and Jager," Morning said in a teasing voice. "And, if you didn't sit there haunting the windows, watching the world walk by, you could come over and say hi when they were here."

"I'd be right over if you told me they were there now."

"And you obviously know they aren't. Otherwise you wouldn't be calling me," she said. Her friend was a man chaser. Yet she was supershy, so she only did her chasing online.

"Well, I could come over now. Maybe they'll come home while I'm there."

"You could do that. Have you eaten?"

"All day long," Nancy said with a groan. "Every time I try a diet, the first thing I do is overeat as if I'm starving."

"You should probably talk to a shrink about that," Morning said with a chuckle.

"Not all of us are blessed to have small trim figures, like you, and no appetite."

"Hey, I eat," Morning protested. "Just not as much as you do."

"I know. How sad is that?"

"Did you get a full-time teaching job yet?"

"No, I was called in for a day of substitution at a downtown school. It's not my favorite place, but the kids are good."

"Midlands High School? The inner-city school?"

"Yeah. I don't know what I'd do if they offered me a full-time job. I'm always conflicted when I go."

"But you're in teaching for the kids' sakes," Morning said. "So, if they offered you a full-time job, then you'd take it."

"Maybe. I've been thinking lately about moving though."

"Moving? Where?" Morning's thoughts had been on the same subject earlier. Not that she had any plans to leave.

"Anywhere," Nancy said passionately. "I feel like I'm not living anymore. I'm just existing. Going through the motions to make it from one day to the next. Nothing ever changes."

"Change starts within. You know that," Morning said.

"Easy for you to say. You've got the house for income

and your art."

"We've been over this before. You're living at your parents' house. You went to school for marketing, and yet you don't want to work in your field."

"No. That's why I switched to teaching," Nancy said patiently. "But, if I can't get a job in my chosen field, I have no income to pay the bills."

"But every day is more experience. Eventually you'll get a full-time teaching position."

"Sure, but, if I went to an area that needed teachers, chances are I could get a job easier."

"Start applying. If you get a job, well, I guess that's where you're going."

Nancy chuckled. "I have my résumé open in front of me. I'm updating it."

Morning felt a jolt to her system. "Wow, then you are serious."

"More so than I have been in a long time."

The two talked a little longer; then Morning ended the call. Yet she spoke to herself out loud. "Nancy, you do love teaching. I don't know why you don't like Midlands High School."

But, of course, Nancy had already hung up. Nancy wouldn't answer that question.

Morning had asked her several times before and always got an answer that some of the teachers were good and that some were kind of creepy. Just like the students.

She'd never heard Nancy talk about students like that before. She'd always been a cheerleader for the kids. So that was already a different take. Still, if her friend did move away, Morning would miss Nancy. And that just brought Morning back to her own fear of losing her home. It might be good for her to move, … to release her father's asset. But doing what was right didn't make it easy.

Just then she heard a vehicle out front. She got up, checked her watch, thought it might be the two men. As she walked toward the front door and opened it, she saw her four o'clock guests had finally arrived, who were now quite late.

The pair came in amid a tumble of exclamations and apologies and luggage.

She smiled and quickly put them at ease. As soon as she got them settled into their room, she said, "You've had a hectic day. If you're hungry, I do have fresh homemade shepherd's pie. I'd be more than happy to serve you some of it."

Both nodded and exclaimed in joy.

Smiling, Morning went downstairs and into the kitchen. She served up two decent-size plates, which still left half the shepherd's pie. Should be enough for the men.

She quickly tossed together a Caesar salad and added place settings to the dining table. When her guests arrived, Bruce and Brenda Carter—and, boy, did she have to smile at those names—they sat down at the table. She brought a cup of coffee over and joined them.

They explained about one of their flights being canceled because of a door that wouldn't seal and how they'd been shunted to another plane and then still another plane and so would be staying longer here at the B&B, if that was okay. They really shouldn't, but, after their rough trip, they felt they deserved a second day.

Morning just nodded. "Traveling these days, it's not always as simple as it's made out to be."

As soon as the couple ate, they headed out, promising they'd be back by eleven as per her rules. Some people didn't like to follow rules. And those individuals she told not to come back. She deliberately wasn't supercheap in her pricing. It was her home she was opening after all. Other places in town were less expensive for an overnight stay, and that worked for her.

She was cleaning up their dishes when she heard a knock at the front door again. She walked toward it, smiling, as she opened it. But there was no one there. Frowning she stepped out and looked around. But there was no sign of anyone. Probably just kids. Stepping back inside, she closed the door then called Geir. "I don't know when you're planning on coming back tonight …"

"Sorry," he responded. "We didn't mean to be this long."

"It doesn't matter," she said. "I'm not trying to check up on you. Just thought I'd let you know that dinner is here for you whenever you get hungry."

"We're at Midlands High School right now," Geir said. "We thought it would still be open but hadn't realized how late it was."

"Staff is often there until five," Morning said. "A friend of mine will work there tomorrow."

"Doing what?"

"She works as a substitute teacher on an on-call basis."

"Any idea why she got called in?"

"Apparently the school just found out one of the teachers has died, so she'll be subbing for that teacher tomorrow."

"We will be there soon," Geir said abruptly and hung up the phone.

"WHAT'S THE CHANCE the guy we found dead in the alley is this teacher who died?"

"It's hard to say." They stood on the school steps, but the doors were locked, and the playground was empty. Garbage blew aimlessly across the parking lot. "There should be a staff directory online."

Geir pulled out his tablet as they walked toward his truck. "We never did get an ID on the dead guy."

"The cops won't release that until the next of kin is notified. So chances are, it's early for the school to have been notified."

Geir nodded. But he couldn't help thinking it was odd to have just heard of a teacher being killed after finding a body. "Unless, of course, Poppy had something to do with it, and he told them."

"Which would be easily verified and not smart on his part."

"I know."

As they walked back through the parking lot, a vehicle came in. Geir and Jager studied it. The driver took one look at them, then bolted out of the parking lot.

"Interesting."

"Could be anything from a parent trying to do a late pickup of a child and is afraid of getting in trouble for having missed them, to somebody looking to score drugs and the dealers have already left the school grounds," Geir said drily.

"True enough."

They stopped at the edge of the parking lot, took one last look at the school. Jager said, "We'll check in again in the morning."

"What about Mason?" Geir asked.

"I doubt Mason knows more than he did at our meeting in Santa Fe before we left."

"True, but I just feel like there should be some names by now."

"He did say the navy found signs of tampering within their personnel database. Names, dates, etc. The navy says the hacking only worked because they were changing their software from an ancient system. The files were placed in the archive system, then automatically updated to the new system, overriding the old files."

"And, if it happened during the systems update, then you would think that the hacking could have been done by a programmer."

"It's possible."

"Right, so we don't know if Mouse was part of that or not."

Jager shook his head. "No, we don't, but a part of me says he may have been because he was terribly incompetent in so many other things."

"He *was* tech-savvy. When Laszlo and I talked to Lance, before someone took him out, Lance told us how Mouse had 'techno guts and brains,' where Lance had the brawn. Yet, despite Mouse's fear of water, he still managed to make it as a SEAL."

"And, of course, that's the next question. *Did he?* What if somebody gave him a pass on his BUD/S training in his file? Add that information to the rest of his record, and he was given a unit to work with. That's a hell of a hacking job, and that's with him making it into the navy on his own. But what if it's more than that? What if he didn't even qualify for the navy, much less the SEALs?"

"Something's majorly wrong with our system when

somebody can fake *any* of that."

Jager stopped and looked at Geir, then asked, "And, of course, along with that disturbing element is, did somebody take out another SEAL so Mouse could take his place?"

"The students came from across the country to pass BUD/S training. There are photo IDs, all kinds of checks and balances to make sure it all works." Jager frowned. "But why? Why go to all that trouble?"

"Because it's what Mouse ultimately wanted and didn't figure he could make it any other way."

The two men stopped beside Geir's truck. Geir could see Jager's rented Jeep Wrangler a few vehicles ahead. Geir shook his head. "It's pretty sad if that's how Mouse got in."

"What about fingerprints?"

Geir said, "Remember? Mouse burnt his fingers badly. The prints would never be comparable to earlier ones. You know yourself we only use our ID tags now. We never have to go through fingerprinting or anything else anymore. My prints were taken when I had my first complete medical examination." Geir turned to face Jager. "So maybe Mouse stole someone else's identity and stepped into the navy. Not going through any of the normal channels."

"You mean, Mouse found someone who had already passed BUD/S training? Then targeted him, and, when an opportunity arose, he took him out?"

"It's possible. You know it is. And, of course, he'd arrive green, wouldn't know anybody, wouldn't have a clue how it all worked. But, because he'd passed, he would have been accepted. All his paperwork, his documentation would have been in order."

Jager leaned his arms atop the truck. "That makes more sense than to think of anybody trying to fake it from the very beginning of the navy induction. Just to get into the navy entails so many background checks and mountains of paperwork and manifold identification confirmations for the initial process. But, if Mouse took out somebody and stepped in after the fact, then the danger was only if anybody was able to identify him as an imposter."

"Exactly. But he'd have to make sure it was a damn close match."

"Or was a close-enough match that a little bit of surgery or a different hairstyle or makeup would do the trick."

They looked at each other.

"Are we really suggesting," Jager said out loud, "that the Mouse we had in our unit could have done something like this?"

"It would explain a lot of things," Geir said slowly. "And I don't want to be speaking ill of the dead if it's not true, but we all know that, even though Mouse had some training, he was terribly inept at so many things."

"And yet he was fit, very physically strong, capable. And we did an awful lot of one-on-one training with him to bring his skills up to snuff."

"But, at the time, we were like, *What the hell? This guy is desperately in need. How had he made it this far?* But we never questioned that maybe he *didn't* make it this far, that maybe something else was going on."

Jager glared at his friend with a hard look. "Why would we? He was a SEAL. He was one of us. And, like everything else we do, if he was one of us, we would help him make it through his weaker areas."

"And we didn't go on many missions with him."

"No, the couple missions we did, one off in Italy and the training mission we did out of Australia, he had a broken leg, didn't he?" Jager asked thoughtfully. "When you think about it, Mouse, who was only with us for that year, wasn't in a position to swim much."

"Considering we spent weeks skydiving, conducted over-the-beach landings and landed via small rubber craft, swimming hadn't been a requirement. In one mission, remember how we had to take down a ship in our own high-speed boats by boarding the ship at night?"

Jager nodded.

"Mouse had been with us all the way. And he'd been in the water—occasionally. But I don't remember seeing Mouse doing more than the bare minimum when it came to swimming. … Of course we weren't looking for any signs of deception back then."

"Shit," said Jager. "It makes my stomach churn to think that's what was going on."

"But we can't jump to conclusions," Geir said. "There could be another explanation."

"Maybe. But I'm not seeing it right now," Jager said quietly.

CHAPTER 4

O N WEDNESDAY, MORNING was up early. She felt bad that the men had missed out on dinner and chose not to charge them for it. Breakfast was included, and she suspected they could make a pretty decent dent in whatever she had. She did up a plateful of sausages, and, as the men came in, she turned with a bright smile. "How do you want your eggs?"

"Sunny-side up," they both said.

She nodded, pointed at the urn and said, "Coffee's ready. Help yourself. I'll have your eggs ready in a minute." She cracked two into the pan and then two more. At the silence behind her, she turned. Both men sat at the eat-in kitchen table and stared at her frying pan. She frowned and said, "Okay, so how many eggs will it take?"

They both grinned. "Another each would be good."

She rolled her eyes. "Typical big healthy males."

They nodded.

She needed a second pan for frying that many eggs, so she filled another pan and then turned to the bread. "Toast?" She pointed to the fresh bread she'd just pulled out of the oven.

"It would be a waste to toast that," Geir said. "But I'll take a slab with butter."

She nodded, and, with a quick glance at the eggs to

make sure they were okay, she walked to the fresh bread and cut off four slices. Jager snagged the crusty end piece.

"Hey, I was gonna grab that," Geir said.

Jager just shrugged. "You were too slow. You've always been too slow."

Geir shot him a look but reached for the butter and slathered the creamy yellow stuff on his bread. Jager didn't seem to mind no butter, at least on the crusty slice. But when he went for the second piece, he buttered it.

As Morning served the eggs and sausages, she shook her head. "Do I need to cut another few slices?"

"Yes, from the other end," Geir grumbled.

She laughed and obliged.

With delighted surprise he accepted the crust she handed him and then smirked at Jager. "Ha, ha."

Jager, in response, grabbed two of the center pieces. He looked at her and said, "Do you have any honey or peanut butter?"

"Oh my, I totally forgot." She walked to the formal dining room table already set and brought back a small tray she kept full of honey, jams and peanut butter for breakfast.

Jager's face lit up. He polished off his sausage and eggs faster than anybody she'd ever seen, whereas Geir ate slowly, savoring bite for bite. By the time he was done with his food, Jager was well into a thickly plastered peanut butter and honey sandwich.

She studied the two men in fascination. "Do you guys eat like this all the time?"

They stopped and stared at her.

She chuckled. "Right, this is just normal." She could hear movement upstairs. "My other guests will be coming down soon."

Geir's gaze narrowed. "How many?"

"Two, a husband and wife. They'll be here all day today, overnight again and leave tomorrow morning."

Geir nodded. "Anybody else coming in?"

"I'm waiting for a family to confirm sometime today when they are due to arrive. They weren't sure if they'd be in Wednesday—today—or Friday, depending on flights. There was an issue with one of them. What are you two up to today?" she asked. "And it occurred to me when I woke up this morning, do you need or want to speak to my friend who'll be working at the school?"

Geir tilted his head and gave a quick nod. "That would be a good idea. Does she get breaks? We only need to meet with her for a few minutes."

Morning nodded. "She does indeed. I'll send her a text and see what she says." She pulled out her phone and sent Nancy a text, asking if she had a moment to speak with the two men at school today.

Nancy's response was an immediate question. **The cute ones?**

Trying to keep her face straight, she replied, **Find out for yourself.**

Sure, I'll have a break between 11:30 and 12:30.

Where can they meet you?

At the office.

Morning looked up and said, "Nancy can meet you between eleven-thirty and twelve-thirty—the earlier the better. She'll meet you at the office."

"Tell her eleven-thirty. And thank her for us."

Morning nodded. "I just confirmed that with her." She brought up Nancy's profile and held up the picture of her friend. "Just so you recognize her."

Both men took a moment to study her friend, whose curvy proportions had often made her very popular with the guys, but they were usually after one thing, according to Nancy. And she wasn't interested if that was all it was. She wanted marriage and two kids in the little white house with the picket fence. She also wanted to stay married for sixty years and grow old in rocking chairs on the front veranda of the same house. She often asked Morning why she wasn't of the same opinion.

So far Morning hadn't had a decent answer. But she figured, if she ever found Mr. Right, she'd take whatever it was Mr. Right had in mind so she could be with him.

She was tied to this place, but she wasn't so tied that she'd walk away from a relationship she believed in 100 percent. She did believe in compromise, but, in the end, she guessed she was a romantic because no way would she walk away from that person who she'd been waiting for all her life.

She glanced at the men as they finished their coffee. "So now that you've tanked up, are you heading to the school?"

Both men shrugged in a noncommittal manner, which she took to mean it was none of her business. She nodded as she swept the plates out from under them. "Have a good day hunting."

That stopped them short. They turned to look at her.

She gave them a bland gaze back. "Obviously you're hunting somebody at the school. I get that. Just stay safe, all right?" Then she beamed. "Besides I have to redeem myself at dinner. If you'll be here for it, that is," she said.

The men stared at her. "Redeem yourself?"

"Sure. You came in to warmed-up plates of shepherd's pie. I pride myself on my cooking," she said by way of explanation. "Now, if you guys can give me a time that you'll be here, I could give you a lovely meal."

Both men looked interested, but it was Geir who said, "Shepherd's pie wasn't lovely?"

"Well sure, but it was pretty bland. And there was no dessert."

Both men's gazes went to the cinnamon buns she had brought out, but only about six were left. She nodded toward them. "If you still have room, go ahead."

Both men reached out and snagged one.

She shook her head. "After this much food for breakfast, you probably won't need anything else until dinner tonight."

"It's always good to be fed when you go hunting," Jager said, mumbling around the food in his mouth.

She nodded. "Exactly as I thought."

Both men, their second cinnamon buns now in hand, disappeared.

She did the dishes, then went to her freezer and pulled out steaks. She had some big prawns she could grill with them. She seasoned the steaks and left them in the fridge to defrost. She'd been planning to do something with them on the weekend, but they could be eaten now. She liked to marinate her meat a little longer if she could.

She walked to the living room and watched through the front window as both men hopped into the truck. She thought it was Geir's truck. Interesting they were only taking one this time.

As she headed past her front counter, the phone rang. She frowned. She wanted to get to her studio. She answered it to find another single male would be arriving. In delight, she told him it was no problem, and she would be here most of the day and could check him in. He said he'd be here within an hour.

"Perfect," she said as she hung up. She had two rooms ready. She thought about it and decided which one it would be. She put a note down in her guest book and went to her studio to make the most of the time she had.

As she walked inside the small studio, turning on the lights and opening up as many of the windows as she could, she deliberately avoided looking at her new painting. Finally, when she couldn't stand it anymore, she stood in front of it and studied it.

And sighed with joy. It was just as amazing as it had been the first time.

Finally she took it down, set it on the floor against the wall, where it would be prominent while she painted the next one. She brought up a slightly larger canvas and put it on the easel. She had no clue what it would be, but it needed to be something in the same vein as the last one. She had to have something, more than one something, for Friday. And she had to have a theme, a name for the collection. She closed her eyes as she thought about it but immediately felt tension choking her. What if she couldn't duplicate the first effort? "Stop that," she chided herself. "It takes trust. And a lot of it. Grab your paints and start like you did yesterday."

To that end, she walked to the sink, pulled out her brushes, dried them off until they were perfect for working with and then headed to her large selection of paints. With her clean palette in hand, she found a beautiful orange, some yellow and some white that she mixed together. It took her a bit to work it in, but suddenly this bright tangerine formed with a weird luminescent glow to it. She smiled happily.

"Perfect." She returned to the canvas, stood in front of it for a moment with her eyes closed, then took a deep breath. "Okay, so this is faith. You need to have a little faith in your ability. Let's go."

And without any real idea of what she was doing, she set her paintbrush and paint to the canvas and started working.

Once again, she got so caught up that, when the doorbell rang, it surprised her. She checked the clock and realized her guest had arrived. She set aside the palette and paintbrushes, tossed off her smock and raced downstairs. She beamed as the businessman walked in. "I presume you're Ken Wiley?"

He nodded his head, and she registered him. "Let me take you to the room."

She led him upstairs and down the hall, putting him in the room across from either Jager or Geir—she never did find out who was in which room. She opened the door and showed the room to Ken.

He nodded politely. "This will be fine. Thank you very much."

She turned to him. "Would you like a cup of coffee? If so, I can go put on a pot."

He shook his head. "I'll be leaving soon. I'll be back later this afternoon or evening," he said thoughtfully. "I'm not exactly sure what time."

"And you're only staying one night?"

He shook his head. "If you don't mind," he said gently, "I'd like to book at least two nights."

She beamed. "That's fine. I'll make a note of it in the guest book. Breakfast is between seven and ten. Just come down whenever you're ready in the morning, and I'll be happy to provide a nice breakfast for you."

He nodded, but he was already putting his briefcase on the bed, opening it to pull out a laptop.

She was amazed how electronic the world had become.

It seemed to her everybody was attached to their cell phone, tablet or laptop. She understood, but, at the same time, she thought the world should unplug for a certain number of hours every day.

With her new guest taken care of, she headed back to her studio and straight to her painting, curious to know exactly what she'd been working on. As she stood there, her breath caught in the back of her throat. She'd done it again. She didn't know what the painting was yet, but she had this interesting orange glow working off the background. And she realized it faded outward, as if coming through a fog. She went with that theme and developed the fog more. But that was only half the canvas. She had to see what was below it first.

She switched to grays and blacks and put in a skyline. As she worked, she stayed focused on that orange light. Several hours later, she stopped, her hands shaking. She'd done all the sky colors in the background, but she still needed to work that light and fog farther over the top. That was the thing about painting; it was always best to do it in layers. You always worked from the background forward, but, in this case, she also needed an overlay of fog. And so that had to be layered on next.

She worked until her phone rang. When she straightened and answered it, she found Nancy on the phone. "Hey, how are you doing?"

"I'm doing great. I met your two guests. They just had a few questions about the school system and how it works, the teachers," Nancy gushed. "Those men are not only gorgeous but they are nice too."

Morning frowned, her mind still half on the painting. She dragged her attention away from the big canvas. "Men?"

Nancy pealed with laughter. "You're painting, aren't you?"

"Well, I was," she confessed. "At least until you interrupted me."

"Well, I'm sorry." Nancy twittered with laughter again. "No, I'm not. You sent those two men to talk to me. You know how gorgeous they are?"

"When did they get there?" Morning asked with a frown. "I thought they would have been there hours ago."

"Silly, it's just eleven-thirty," Nancy said. "Actually it's eleven-fifty," she corrected. "Remember? We set it up for eleven-thirty."

She shrugged. "Right, I forgot about that. They left the house hours ago, so I lost track of time."

"When you're in your painting zone," Nancy said firmly, "everything gets lost. But particularly time."

"That may be," Morning said quietly as she stared at her painting, "but I've started a couple paintings that are … unique."

"Is *unique* good?" Nancy asked cautiously.

It was Morning's turn to laugh. "It's always good."

"Great. Anyway, I have to go and get some lunch before I'm back in class again. Have fun painting." And she hung up.

The trouble was, Morning had been pulled out just enough that it broke the magic. But, on the other hand, it was past lunchtime, and she needed to eat something herself. She carefully set her painting materials to the side, took one last look at the very odd light on the canvas and smiled. "This just might work."

She headed to the kitchen. As she went, she thought, "So what the hell were those men up to this morning if they just now got to the school?"

None of my business. She might be curious, but they sure as hell weren't going to share. It just wasn't part of their nature.

GEIR WALKED THROUGH the hallways of the second floor of the school. They'd already done a full check of the neighborhood, the parks and the men who worked at the school. Geir and Jager had a good idea of who they might be looking for. There were three options. The other teachers weren't in the right age category or nationality. After checking police records in Texas on Poppy's fetish with little boys, the general consensus was white/late 40-50s, yet he'd somehow escaped capture.

"Nancy is an interesting character," Jager said. "She's knowledgeable about the school but hasn't been here long enough to know much about the teachers."

Geir looked at him with a grin. "Interested?"

Jager shook his head. "No."

Geir shrugged. "You could do worse."

"Maybe, but Morning is more my style."

"Morning Blossom? Really?" Geir frowned, not liking the sound of that at all. He had just met the woman though, so he didn't know why he'd be pissed off—if that was the case here. He should be happy for Jager. "Go for it then."

Jager laughed. "Like you'd let me."

Geir stopped at the top of the stairs leading to the first floor and turned to look at him. "Why wouldn't I?" His tone was a bit challenging. He frowned. What the hell? ... It shouldn't matter to him who Jager saw.

Jager smiled, smacked him on the shoulder and said, "Go ahead and pretend you don't care, but I can already see the interest."

"Hey, she's pretty. She can cook. She's nice. There'd be something wrong with me if I didn't respond to that."

"I agree totally," Jager said. "She's also a friend of Mason's, and he'd be happy to give you the rundown."

"Oh, no. No rundown, thank you very much. And definitely not from Mason. It'd be all over the bloody group before too long if that were the case."

"Nah, Tesla would just think another one had bitten the dust."

"Not happening," Geir said. "At least not until this nightmare is over."

"We are getting closer," Jager said. "If we can track down this Poppy and find out what the hell happened to Mouse on this end, I think it could blow the whole thing wide open."

"Maybe. I'm just not so sure at this point. We've tracked this asshole all over the world."

"But then our life was all over the world. We've lived a global lifestyle because we were in the navy. It was hard to see it as anything other than normal. But, once you're outside, you realize just how much of a tight community the navy was and how completely different the world is apart from the navy environment."

"I was thinking about that," Geir said. "It's like a before and after. We had our life before the accident, and now we have a life afterward. But I can't say I'm all that comfortable with this one yet."

"That's because we were kingpins in the other one," Jager said. "We were at the top of the top, the best of the best and all that crap. But one land mine dropped us right to the bottom."

"And so damn fast," Geir said. "I wasn't ready to leave active duty."

"I hear you. But I'm sure as hell not taking a desk job."

"Exactly. How do you go to something so much less than what you were?"

"I don't think you do," Jager said. "I think you're supposed to move on, to find something else, to find something different, to find something that suits our new world."

"Not doing so well with that," Geir said. "Can't say that you look to be doing so well either."

Jager chuckled. "No, I'm not sure I am, but that doesn't mean we can't. I think we're just stuck. All of us waiting for this to sort itself out."

"We still need to be thinking forward, finding something we want to do, that we can do after this."

"What about starting a company, like Levi's?" Jager asked. "I've been wondering about something along that line. It doesn't have to be quite so physical, considering our injuries, and we could take on some jobs from him if they happened to be in our part of the world. He's certainly overworked."

Geir stopped and stared at Jager. They were now outside, standing on the front steps of the school. Just as he was about to say something, the bell overhead rang, deafening both of them. When it finally stopped, he said, "I'd forgotten how much I hate school bells."

Jager chuckled. They hopped down the steps easily, making sure they were out of the way before the kids either came tearing out or went running inside. Geir and Jager escaped through the front gates and stood beside Geir's truck. Geir wondered about Jager's suggestion. "What kind of work will we do though?"

"We can do either security work or bodyguard work. Or we could do investigative work."

"Like PIs?"

"I don't want to pigeonhole it into that," Jager said. "Levi built himself a very large company, and it's doing very well. We don't have to go big. We can stay small with just the seven of us. Make it something we can handle with our growing families, not work so hard and so crazy, but potentially have something to bring in an income."

They hopped into the truck and sat there thinking for a few moments. Geir turned his attention back to the school. "Interesting that two of the three men we were looking for didn't show up for work today. That there's a Joel Henderson and a Reginald Henderson added to the confusion."

Jager nodded. "I was just thinking that. Wonder if the homeless men put out the word that Poppy was being hunted."

"I wouldn't be at all surprised. Get paid from him too for their information. The question is, how do we run Poppy to ground?"

"Well, the school didn't give us any personnel information, but we do have their full names. We should be able to research them easily enough."

While they sat here, both men brought out their laptops and got to work. But the space was cramped. Geir looked at Jager. "Surely a coffee shop is somewhere close by."

Jager nodded and hit Google Maps. "Two blocks ahead, take a left and its right there."

"Good enough." Geir turned on the truck. He followed the directions and pulled into the back of the parking lot.

They hopped out and walked inside. Each ordering a coffee, they went to a table at the very back of the busy place and sat down with their laptops side by side.

"I also didn't see him on the staff photo wall, did you?"

"No, I didn't."

Sipping their coffee, they did whatever public research they could access from where they were sitting. For more than that—like access to tax forms and medical records—they'd have to get some authorized assistance. It wasn't that they didn't know where and how, but they needed access to databases they didn't currently have.

Geir lifted his head at one point, looked around and said, "*This* is what we can do …"

Jager nodded. "It is. We're a little less physical than what we used to be, but we're in very good shape, and it's not like we can't do a more physical job if it comes through. The other thing is, if we do get a bigger job or something that's up Levi's alley, we can always subcontract out with them."

"Or hire a couple of his men to work for us," Geir said. "We're better off doing it that way and getting the fee ourselves."

Jager studied his buddy for a long moment, then nodded. "True enough. You're excellent at cracking safes—in fact, anything that's locked. I'm good at walking in the shadows."

"I'm also good at walking in shadows. But you're better," Geir said magnanimously. "You're amazing at disappearing into the woodwork." The two men went back to their research, but Geir's mind wouldn't leave him alone. "We could hire a manager."

Jager nodded. "That would probably be best."

"Unless you like doing bookkeeping, paperwork, tax

filings," Geir said, teasing.

Jager shot him a horrified look. "I couldn't stand handing in navy reports. No way you're tying me to a desk job."

Geir stopped teasing and got serious. "Apparently Joel Henderson lives on Morrison Road." Geir turned the screen so Jager could see what he'd found.

Jager leaned over to read the article. "It just says Morrison Road but doesn't give the actual number. We should check him in the online phone book listings." Jager ran it down and said with triumph, "Five five two five."

"Good. I'll write that down. Now let's track Reginald Henderson. Maybe we can drive past their houses this afternoon." After a moment, he added, "How does a pedophile operate like this all these years without detection?"

"Teacher," Jager said simply. "A position of trust with easy access to the kids."

Geir nodded. "But how is it none of the other adults knew?"

"Because somehow he had a hold over the kids, so nobody ever told."

"But that's victim profiling to the nth degree," Geir said. "In order to pick up a victim like that, Poppy has to know exactly what his target needs. In that way Poppy can ensure he fills that need so the kid feels completely loyal and indebted to Poppy for providing that one thing the kid thinks he must have."

"Which is exactly what he did with Mouse—helped him become Ryan."

"Any chance he's the one who killed Mouse? Maybe Mouse wasn't suitably grateful? Or something ... Maybe Mouse wanted to ditch Poppy after Mouse did make it? A lover's tiff?"

Just then Jager popped up with Reginald Henderson's address. "Here we go. Got an address for both now."

They shut down their laptops, took their coffee cups back to the front counter and walked out to the parking lot.

"Maybe Mouse finally got away from Poppy, saw just how damaging the sexual predation was and threatened to turn him in."

Jager stopped and looked at Geir. "In a way that makes more sense than anything we've heard so far. But how would Poppy have known the accident would kill only Mouse?"

"Well, that's the thing, isn't it? Maybe he didn't care. Maybe, as long as he got Mouse, Poppy was totally happy if we all went too."

Jager nodded. "I could see that. But it's extreme. Especially when those winos claimed Poppy wasn't a killer. He was a wimp, a beggar. But he could have easily hired somebody to do the dirty jobs."

With Geir driving, they headed to Joel Henderson's address. They parked across the road and watched a man, his wife and two young children playing out in the front yard. The man pulled out a big handkerchief and blew his nose. He sat down and said, "Honey, I may have to go back inside and lie down."

She placed her hand on his forehead. "You're running a fever again. Maybe you should." She looked worried, and it was evident in her tone, even from where Geir and Jager sat.

Geir turned on the engine and drove away. "It might be him, but chances are it's not."

Jager nodded. "Doesn't seem likely."

They pulled onto the main highway. The second teacher's address was a more run-down-looking house in a decrepit section of town. It was barely respectable, not all that nice.

Geir pulled off to the side of the road and said, "Aren't we close to the address Badger found for Mouse here in San Diego?"

"We're about six blocks away. From here to there, it gets nastier."

"So, close enough to do the fishing he wanted, to provide a home, and yet to keep the young man close to his own home. Close enough but just far enough away."

"Exactly. Mouse probably wouldn't have been thrilled with high living. He would have become very jealous if this guy had been in a massive house with obvious wealth. But here? It's like he was a step above, a step Mouse could easily see himself making."

"Adding in the father-figure persona, and it was almost like going home," Geir said. "Mouse wouldn't have remembered his stepfather too much as he was so young, and, even if he did, the memories wouldn't likely be wonderful as the guy and his mom split soon afterward."

"Did we ever get any information on him? The stepfather, I mean."

Jager shook his head. "Not much. Other than the fact that he knows nothing and wants to know nothing. He didn't have anything helpful to add about Mouse."

"Well, that's getting information. Just not the kind we were hoping for. And apparently there is no way to confirm who was Mouse's father."

Jager nodded. He stared at the empty house and said, "What do you think?"

Geir turned the engine on again, pulled out into the small street and said, "I think we need to do a couple laps around the block. Then a little B&E."

Three times around the block later, he found a parking spot one block over, where he parked, locked up the truck and they headed back to the house. This time for a much closer look.

CHAPTER 5

A S SOON AS Morning made herself a salad, she decided she would take it out on the deck to eat. Her mind was consumed with her two recent paintings. Taking a cup of tea with her, she sat in the sunshine and smiled. A lot was right with her world. Also a lot wasn't so right, but, hey, this was good. Scrambling for a living or working a nine-to-five job wasn't up her alley. But this, the bed-and-breakfast, helped a lot. Her rates were high enough to keep her solvent but still giving her a lot of return customers. It just wasn't full-time. Maybe that was a good thing.

As she sat here, she could feel an eerie sensation, as if somebody watched her. She looked around the backyard. Sometimes neighbor kids would stare through the holes in the fence at her, but it was a school day and during school hours, and there was no sign of them. She looked behind her, but no one was there.

Slightly unnerved but throwing it off, she finished her salad and sat for a few minutes, thinking about the gallery showing. How many was a reasonable number of sample paintings to take in? How many did she have time to do? She had one and a half to date. But today was Wednesday, so she barely had a couple more days. *Four?* "I want four to take in," she determined.

She found that, if she set goals and labeled them as such

out loud, she'd do her best to reach them. And, if she fell short, three would still do. It would give her something to work toward. She didn't have a clue how many she needed to have for the actual showing. And she didn't want to put that kind of pressure on herself right now. She had enough to worry about.

Still unnerved at that strange sense of being watched, she stood, took her plate and cup back inside, rinsed them and loaded the dishwasher. She decided it was full enough, and she turned it on. The couple this morning had chosen to go out for breakfast, so she hadn't had to worry about them.

She headed back up to her studio. She should be doing paperwork in the office, but she needed the studio work time. As she walked in, she realized how strong the paint smell was. She opened the windows wider, trying to get fresh air recirculating through the room. By rights she needed a workshop that was properly vented. But, since that wouldn't happen anytime soon, she'd take what she could. She turned back around to the canvas and heard footsteps in the hall. She glanced up to see her new guest. "This room is out of bounds," she said firmly. "You have your bedroom, the living room downstairs and the kitchen."

He smiled apologetically. "I'm sorry. I just wondered if there was any chance of getting that offer of coffee."

"Of course." She beamed and motioned him to the stairway. "I'm surprised you knew where I was."

"I saw you come up here earlier," he said with a laugh. "And now I see it's an art studio."

"Yes, I do like to paint."

For some reason she didn't want to say anything about the showing. What if they didn't like her work?

In the kitchen she put on a small pot of coffee. "I was

thinking you'd be gone all day," she said, turning to smile at him.

He nodded. "I've been waiting for phone calls. I had a business conference online," he confessed. "That ran long, so, when I do go out, I won't be back until later this evening."

"No problem as long as you remember eleven is curfew."

He chuckled. "Got it."

As soon as the coffee was done, she poured him a cup, then poured herself a cup. "There's still a cup left if you decide you want a second one. I'll see you later then." She turned and walked back out.

She smiled to herself. She was lucky to meet so many interesting people. She'd never been nervous in her own house. Mason had made a point of telling her that she should beef up security, and she had to a certain extent. But she'd never been afraid here. It was home, and she liked that. Still, having the guest come into her private space, at least to the door, had unnerved her.

Returning to her studio she put her coffee down to study her painting. Then walked back to the door, closed and locked it. Having Geir inside yesterday hadn't bothered her. Maybe because he'd so obviously enjoyed seeing her paintings. At least the new one. Yet Ken's presence had been an intrusion. One she hadn't liked.

She walked onto the balcony of her room and took several deep cleansing breaths. The house had all these small little Juliet balconies off every second- and third-floor room. They were barely big enough to hold a chair, but they provided a lot of fresh air. She sat with her coffee for a moment. And then determined not to waste any more time. She went back inside, picked up her paintbrush and got back to it. Because of the cityscape in the front, the lighting had to be perfect. And this one would take longer than the first one in the series.

Finally her grandfather's clock chimed four p.m., and she thought she'd done as much as she could for the day. Plus, the natural light had decreased, and she needed that for this particular style of painting. She stepped back, wiping her hands on her smock. It was good, but it wasn't perfect yet. She still needed to work on some of that light and fog.

She hesitated, wanting to stay a little longer, but, between the loss of light and the fact dinner would be late, she knew she had to go.

She thought she heard a sound downstairs. She opened the door and walked out to the front near her bedroom where she could see if the men had arrived. But there was no sign of Geir's truck. But then she had other company as well. Making a fast decision, she went back to her studio, feeling like a child playing hooky, and set about working on the corner of the canvas that bothered her in particular. It just needed a little more black here, a little more gray there. And before long she was lost again. When she straightened up, she realized she'd been leaning forward intently.

An odd light filled her studio as the sun had set. Now she knew it was late. She closed the windows by half, reminding herself to shut them before night settled in, and then walked out of the room. Realizing she'd left her smock on, she stopped. With a laugh, she pulled it over her head, put it back in the room, and then closed and locked the studio from the outside. She couldn't remember the last time anybody had gone in. But now she'd had two men who had tracked her up here.

She ran lightly down the stairs to see the couple had

come in. They all smiled and exchanged greetings. They were just here to get changed before heading out for the evening.

She walked into the kitchen and pulled out the steaks, seasoned them a little more, drained the juice off the platter and brought out the shrimp. They'd been marinating all day too. With that done, she thought about dessert and realized she had time for a quick cheesecake. She pulled out the cream cheese and whipping cream. Few people realized just how fast cheesecake was to make. If they knew, they'd make it all the time.

But did she have any fruit? And then she remembered the blueberries in the fridge. Before long she had the ingredients ready to go into the pan. She decided instead to put them into small terrines, so they were individual servings. With that done, she put them on a cookie sheet and back into the fridge.

She turned and realized it was going on six. How many people were still in the house? Anybody? She had no way to know. But until Geir and Jager returned, she didn't want to go forward with grilling the steaks. She could do something about the potatoes though. She scrubbed them, sliced them very thinly, mixed them with cream, cheese and a quick butter sauce and put them in the oven.

They would take an hour, but hopefully the men would get back in perfect timing. All that was left were the almond-topped green beans. Wandering the house, she wondered why she decided these men needed dinner. It was an invitation she rarely gave to other guests. But then something about Geir and Jager had her wanting to spend more time with them. Especially Geir.

She walked into her office and got down to work. At

least this way she'd keep an eye on the front door.

As she sat, she realized she'd left her phone here. She picked it up to see several text messages from Geir. She smiled as she hit Dial. When he answered, she said, "I'm sorry. I was upstairs painting."

"That's fine. You're not at our beck and call by any means. I called earlier to tell you that we're running a bit late."

"Well, you're not here, so that makes sense." She laughed.

"We're only a couple blocks away, so we'll be there soon."

She hung up and returned to the kitchen to turn up the oven temperature, hoping to expedite the potatoes. That's when she saw a stranger walking through her backyard. She stepped out on the deck and called out, "Hey!"

Large evergreens were in the back corner. He disappeared behind them. She frowned. "You're on private property. Leave please."

She did have trouble with some people in the neighborhood, but generally it was a very safe family-oriented location. She slipped down the deck steps and headed to the back corner. Mason would tell her to stop immediately, but she'd never been one to avoid confrontation if necessary. But, when she got there, she found no sign of anyone. She walked through the small treed area and frowned. "Hello?"

No answer.

Shrugging, she headed back to the house. As she started up the deck steps, she peered into the shadows of the back corner and swore she could see somebody, despite just being there and finding no one. She walked back into the kitchen, laughing at herself. "I must be imagining things. But why now?" she asked herself. "Why today?"

"Why what?" Geir asked.

With a start she spun.

He gave her a lazy smile that set her heart pounding.

"Don't turn that lethal smile on me," she warned.

His eyebrows shot up. "*Lethal?*" he asked with interest.

She snorted. "Like you don't know."

"I really don't. Tell me more," he said, walking closer.

She chuckled. "Where's Jager?"

"Oh, so it's Jager now, is it? Not me? My heart is broken, you know that?" he said with a laugh.

She rolled her eyes at him. "Not likely. And you guys did get here quickly."

"Told you that we were just a couple blocks away."

"Any luck hunting?"

"No. The person we were looking for wasn't at home."

"Sorry. Come on." She turned back to him. "Are you ready for dinner? Or are you going out?"

He pointed at the steak and prawns in front of her. "I'm not going anywhere if that's what we're having for dinner."

She chuckled. "It is indeed."

He glanced at his clothes. "In that case, I'll grab a quick shower, if Jager is done."

"You don't need to wait. I've got an extralarge hot water tank."

He raised his eyebrows again. "Perfect. I'll be back in five." And he slipped out just as silently as he'd slipped in.

She crossed her arms and thought about that. It was one thing to have guests around the house, but it was another to find so many men who could move as silently as they did. She turned to the copse of trees in the backyard because that was exactly how whoever she'd seen moved. Could it have been Jager or Geir? No, she would have recognized them. But, then again, she hadn't exactly gotten a good look at her intruder. She didn't want to consider that Ken might have been the man skulking in the backyard as that meant she was questioning everyone around her. Not the way she wanted to live.

Pushing the issue to the back of her mind, she checked on the potatoes and found they'd started to bubble. She turned the oven down slightly and returned to her paperwork. Until the men came down, no point in putting the steaks on the grill. And the prawns? Well, they took even less time to cook.

She settled down happily, a smile on her face thinking about Geir's smile. There was something about it. Just the corners kicked up, but it tugged a response from her that she hadn't felt in a long time.

She'd had several boyfriends, but they always seemed to be more interested in her house and the property than her. One had wanted to move into one of the bedrooms on a permanent basis. When she explained she needed all the bedrooms for income, he'd been quite disturbed, to the point she had to call a friend to help escort him out. She hadn't seen him since. That had been only a few months ago. At the time she'd been affronted at his forwardness, but Nancy had put it in perspective. She'd said, "You have to understand that anybody who doesn't have what you have looks at this and sees revenue and a home, and, because you cook, it's perfect. This is a family home. This is all one needs wrapped up into one."

"But only for me," Morning had said. "As far as I'm concerned, he was just a user."

"Oh, I agree. But, if you look at it from his perspective,

being Johnny-on-the-spot and getting free rent, it would have been a pretty damn good deal."

"He only got one night out of it. Once I realized he didn't plan on leaving, I kicked him out of here."

"And that's because of your generous heart," Nancy said. "You'd give anybody a bed for the night. The trouble is, you never do any background checks to see if they're upstanding citizens."

"Like a background check will tell me that," Morning scoffed.

Nancy nodded, chuckled and said, "True enough. All of my boyfriends would have passed a background check, yet I definitely know how to pick the losers."

"And I'm not picking them at all," Morning said. "Can't say any of the relationships I've had have been any better."

"No. And for a different reason," Nancy said. "People look at my house and think it's mine without realizing it's my parents' and, when they realize it's my parents', they don't want anything to do with me. In your case, it is your house—at least half of it is. So that becomes a huge checkmark on the side of right."

"Until they realize I run a bed-and-breakfast, and people will always be around."

"Exactly."

Morning left her past thoughts, finished the accounts and walked back into the kitchen. There she found Ken. "Ready to head out, are you?"

Ken turned, his movement smooth and silent, just like Geir and Jager. Was he ex-military too?

"Absolutely." He smiled at her.

His smile was cheerful and bright, which was nice.

"I just wanted to say goodbye. I'll be back later tonight."

She walked with him to the front door.

He patted her shoulder gently and said, "Take care." And he walked down the steps with a light tread and a whistle.

She smiled and called out, "Have a good evening."

He raised a hand in goodbye.

She watched as he went to the corner, looking for whatever vehicle he drove. She had parking for six here, but often the neighbors took them up, making it a struggle at times. Then she smiled when he got into a Porsche, a black one, and disappeared around the corner.

She closed the door and turned around, returning to the kitchen. There Jager sat at the table, his laptop open. He lifted his head and said, "I'm home. Something smells good."

"It's dinner. As soon as I know Geir is ready, I'll light the barbecue and put on the steaks."

Jager lifted his gaze, grinned at her and said, "Or you could just do it now, and Geir might lose out."

She rolled her eyes at him. "That's not likely to happen in my house." But she went out and lit the barbecue. Because, if she understood men, that smell would get Geir down here faster than anything.

GEIR MADE HIS way to the kitchen. He could hear sounds of somebody else in one of the other rooms. He had to wonder just how busy she was here. He'd never thought to ask how many rooms she could fill at one time. But, if she charged a couple hundred a night per room, she had to be making a decent income. He was happy for her, particularly if her true love was her painting. It was hard enough as an artist to make a go of it, and everyone needed to have some kind of a backup plan. In her case, the bed-and-breakfast appeared to suit her admirably.

He walked into the kitchen, sniffing the air. "I smell barbecue," he said.

Jager chuckled. "She said, if she lit it, it would bring you down faster than anything."

Geir smiled. "She's very easy to get along with."

"She is," Jager said with a grin.

Just then Morning stepped into the kitchen. "There you are. I figured you'd be ready for food soon."

"How are you cooking the steaks?"

"Medium-rare for me. I was about to ask how you guys like yours."

"Medium-rare for both of us."

She disappeared back outside again, and, before long, they were all sitting down to a fantastic dinner. She'd set the outside table. "It's just the three of us for dinner."

"Do you normally do dinners?" Jager asked.

"No. Only on special request."

When dinner was over, she cleaned off the patio table, put on a pot of coffee and brought out the cheesecakes.

Geir and Jager had deliberately not told her about their plans. After all, they could hardly say they were planning to go back out to break into a house. They had tried to access it the first time around. But the neighbors had been outside the entire time. Geir and Jager had made sure they hadn't been seen, but neither could they take the chance somebody would come over. They'd decided to defer their inside visit until later in the evening.

When they were finished with their coffee and cheese-cake, the two men stood and smiled at her, and Geir said,

"We have plans, so we can't sit around."

She shook her head. "You came for a reason. Head out and do it. You're not here to entertain me." She grinned, stood to follow the men inside.

Geir smiled, took their coffee cups inside and said, "Maybe not but it's very pleasant here."

"It is," she agreed.

"Have you lived here all your life?"

She shrugged. "Mostly. My father owns half the place. I'm not sure what my future will bring, so this is good for now."

He nodded. "Backup plans are always helpful."

She chuckled. "You didn't say where you're going. I'm not trying to pry …"

He shrugged. "We have a few more people to check up on."

She nodded. "Okay. Sounds good."

Geir turned to look at Jager and said, "You ready?"

He nodded. They escaped the house quickly.

JAGER WAS LAUGHING. "I get that you want to stay in and want to know her a little more."

Geir shrugged. "It's not what I came for."

"Sometimes plans have to change," Jager said. "I can do this alone."

Geir shot him a look and shook his head. "No, I'm part of this. If I get to spend a little time with Morning, then I do. If I don't, then I don't," he said dismissively. And yet inside he knew that would be a shame. He could always come back if he wanted to. But he knew he wouldn't. A lot of memories were here, and, like Jager, Geir had his own mix of good and bad. This had been their home for many years, back when they were whole, ... healthy. A lifetime ago. And yet only a few years ago.

They hopped into his truck, and Geir headed back toward the second man's house. "What's this guy's name again?"

"Reginald Henderson supposedly, but there's no reason he didn't change his name for whatever reason. Easy enough for guys to do. The real question is, is this San Diego guy also the Poppy who Minx knew in Texas? Is this the same person as the Poppy in Texas who Agnes knew as JoJo Henderson???"

At the house, the two men parked around the block and got out. Dusk had just settled. It was a little earlier than they would have liked for their B&E. They walked around the block several times and then headed to another block, comparing neighborhoods.

"It goes downhill within a couple blocks from here," Geir commented.

"Right, which means, an awful lot of potential victims are close by."

"But he wouldn't need to have another stomping ground. He's a schoolteacher, for God's sake. That should give him plenty of choices."

"Sure, but you don't know how long he's owned this house."

"Actually I do. Thirty-seven years," Geir said.

"Wow, that's a long time. So he's got to be closer to sixty than in his late forties. Plus, maybe this is where he started his hunting grounds."

"Possibly. He inherited it from his parents."

"Thirty-seven years ago?"

Geir nodded. "His parents were attacked by an intruder and shot. Their murders remain cold cases."

Jager stopped, turning to look at his buddy. "What?"

"Well, look at the area," Geir said. "Just think about how much crime there has to be. And this was a long time ago. I doubt the neighborhood was a whole lot different back then, but it wouldn't have had the population it has now."

"We should take a look at that murder file," Jager said thoughtfully. "What's the chance this guy killed his parents in order to get the house, so he could carry on with his questionable relationships?"

"It's possible. But is it really probable?"

Jager chuckled. "This guy has stayed in the shadows for a long time. Who knows what he's managed to get away with? Where did that life of crime start? And does he have any other family?"

"There was a younger brother," Geir said. "He committed suicide a couple to three years before the parents were murdered."

"Any idea how much younger?"

"Almost ten years," Geir stated. "Reginald was twenty-five, graduating with a teaching degree, somewhere around the same time his parents were killed. And his brother committed suicide before that. It could have been the reason Reginald ended up going into education."

"It's possible the younger brother committed suicide because his older brother was already working on him as his first victim."

They walked in silence, contemplating a broken family to the extent that maybe this pedophile had abused his younger brother and then murdered his parents to gain the house.

"The trouble is," Jager said, "I hate to even contemplate what the younger brother's life was like, but it does make sense."

"I wonder if somebody could let us know more about both cases. But how would we even find information on the brother's suicide?"

"I searched online but found nothing. Unless the police are willing to share, that information might be available in the newspapers back then. But the suicide would have been about forty years ago."

They turned and headed back toward Reginald's house, finding it still empty, still in darkness. "It almost looks deserted," Geir said.

"I was thinking that myself. What's the chance he has a second home?"

"I would imagine the odds are pretty good, but then why keep this?"

"Maybe for the memories. Maybe for the history here. Maybe to lure his victims here. Who knows?"

Having already cased the place earlier, they knew exactly where their entry point was. They slipped over the back fence from the neighbor's yard, walked through the hedge, sticking to the shadows, something they were both particularly good at, and slinked up to the side of the house. A large window on the bottom floor wasn't locked. Slipping on gloves first, Geir slid it open and was inside in seconds. Jager, after a quick glance around, joined him.

They left the window open to make sure they had an exit. But, if the house was deserted, then any lights they used would be noticed by the neighbors. They couldn't take that chance. They both stood in silence, listening to the sounds, the creaks, the atmosphere of a house that hadn't been lived in, seemingly for a while. There was an odor, one that was hard to distinguish.

"Rats?" Jager whispered.

Geir shrugged. "In this place that would be possible. But is it something else? Who knows?" He turned on his cell phone flashlight and gave the room a quick cursory glance.

Mildew and some dampness. The room they were in was empty. They quickly went through several other rooms on the first floor, but they too were empty. The final door was closed, but, so far, they hadn't heard any sounds of footsteps coming from the house. So Geir had to assume this part behind the closed door was empty too.

Of course that assumption could change at any second. He gently turned the knob and opened the door. They stepped into a small hallway between the kitchen and the living room. They did a walk-through of the living room first, finding standard living room furniture but older and in a rough state. The couch sagged in the middle; an armchair had the corner shredded, possibly by a cat, or possibly just a piece of furniture that he found in the garbage that served the purpose and came home with him.

What it didn't look like was the home of a respectable teacher. No blankets or sheets were thrown over the furniture to say the owners were planning on being gone for a long time. But then, outside of a high-end home, Geir had never seen that before either.

They did a sweep of this part of the main floor and came back to the kitchen. They paused as there was no food, no dishes. Jager put a hand on the refrigerator and whispered, "It's on." He slipped to the side and pulled it open. Horrible smells wafted toward them. He slammed it shut and said,

"Food spoiling."

Uneasy and not sure what was going on, the men made their way to the stairs going to the top floor. The odor was even worse here. With hard looks at each other, they slid upstairs soundlessly. But they already knew what they would find. They just didn't know who. Two bedrooms should be upstairs and a bathroom.

They checked the bathroom first, finding it empty. It wasn't clean, but it wasn't disgusting. They'd certainly seen worse. The smaller bedroom was just an empty room, nobody there. But, oddly enough, a child's toy was in the far corner—a stuffed mouse from the looks of it. Instead of heading straight to the master bedroom, Geir stepped inside and took a quick look but from a child's point of view. And saw crayons and scribble marks on the walls.

Other families had lived here maybe? Did the teacher himself have a family? They hadn't found any record of a marriage or of him having children. But that didn't mean much. He could have had a relationship with somebody who already had a child. The stuffed toy stood incongruently amid the rest of the room. Maybe it was the bright gray new look to it against the old dilapidated color of these surroundings. Maybe it was the cheerful, hopeful smile on the mouse's face. As if it didn't realize it was living in a world that had it seriously in for him.

With a shake of his head, Geir stepped back into the hall.

Jager glanced at him, one eyebrow raised. "What about that bothers you?"

"That it's even here. Why? Surely if he abused children here, the neighbors would have heard the screams?"

"It's hard to say. The house next to it is empty. The

house on the other side is brand new. So just construction workers would have been around for a long time."

"And then, of course, if he had drugged them, nobody would be screaming."

Jager nodded, his jaw tight, his lips pinched.

Side by side the two approached the master bedroom. Of course the door was closed. And Geir already knew he wouldn't like what was on the other side. The odor was much stronger the closer they got. With a gloved hand, he turned the knob, pushing open the door, and the horrible decay smell doubled. They coughed and choked for a moment and then stepped inside. No longer worried about anybody coming in and finding them, Geir turned on the flashlight and shone it toward the bed. A corpse—probably weeks, possibly months old—lay on the bed. No real way to know how long at this point. It had almost mummified.

"That's not good," Jager said.

They walked cautiously forward, trying to identify the victim. But, with the condition of the skin, it was hard. What they could determine was that it was male.

"Old, young?"

Both shook their heads.

"Could be anybody. I'm tempted toward saying young, but I don't have any reason for that," Jager said. He stood and studied the scene for a long moment. "There are no clothes. The bedding is pulled back, as if he was just lying there, and I'm not seeing any major trauma to show he was murdered."

"Well, it can't be our teacher because he still works at the school."

"And he was there several days ago," Jager added.

Geir shook his head. "No, this body's been here too

long." Just as he was about to turn away, he stopped and shone the flashlight over the chest of the victim. "Look at this."

Jager walked closer, and his breath caught in the back of his throat. "So, let me amend that. Definitely murder."

In the chest cavity was a glint of steel—a knife, the hilt broken off and just the edge showing above the ribs.

"So we have a murder victim who's been here for weeks or months in a house that's desolate and run-down, yet the power is on, and the fridge is still running."

"A renter? Maybe the teacher has no idea he's dead?"

"It's hard to say. Obviously the teacher has another place to live himself."

Just then they heard footsteps downstairs.

Grim-faced they slipped against the master door, closing it almost to the point of latching it, and waited.

CHAPTER 6

M ORNING WANDERED THROUGH the kitchen, feeling
suddenly odd. The men were heading to God-only-
knew-where. They were almost secretive about their actions.
Not as in criminal or anything. But just something was off.
She didn't know a better way to describe it.

Unsettled, she realized the house was probably empty,
but she couldn't be sure because, if guests came in and went
up to their rooms when she'd been painting, she wasn't sure
she would have heard them. She walked upstairs to the
second floor and down the hall to the far window. From
there she walked up to the third floor. The rooms up here
were only used for overflow, as they connected to her room
on the other side with the new addition.

But she often walked this way just to make sure everything was okay. She hadn't assigned any of these rooms to
anybody this week, so she took a moment to stop and open
doors, checking out the inside of both rooms. At the far end,
she opened her bedroom door and walked inside.

She closed it behind her and went to the small couch she
kept as a sitting area and collapsed on it. She was out of
sorts, but she was at odds with herself too. She wanted to
paint, and yet something about that made her nervous too.
Fear of failure? Fear of success? She didn't know but figured
the self-help gurus would have a heyday with her. But lying

here and staring moodily at the windows as the darkness settled in wouldn't help either.

And that was, of course, one of the reasons why she struggled with her painting. She did much better in natural light, which was rapidly disappearing.

She heard footsteps down below. Somebody was either coming or going. Normally that didn't bother her in the least, and it certainly shouldn't tonight. If anything, she felt safe with these three single men in the place.

They were all here for their different reasons, either business or otherwise, and that had nothing to do with her as long as no criminal activities went down under her roof.

Still moody, she got up, tried to find a book she wanted to read and gave up. She stood in the middle of her small sitting room, thought about turning on the TV and shook her head. "What I want is to paint."

She headed to her studio, entered and shut the door behind her, flicking on the lights. She assessed the lighting and realized it sucked. But, even if she brought in more lamps, it wouldn't give her the same quality of illumination as the sun did, which she particularly needed for this painting. The trouble was, the unsettled feeling inside her wanted an outlet. Carefully she took her half-finished painting off the easel and put it on the floor, leaning it up against the wall beside the other one. She grabbed an old canvas and stuck it on the easel. She'd done this often a few years ago. Thankfully she hadn't had that sensation since, but now there was this weird feeling she couldn't put words to.

With a sigh she grabbed red paint and a paintbrush and turned back to the canvas. "Okay, this is your chance to work it out. Do whatever you need to do."

She started with big broad slashes across the canvas. Surprised, but already having condemned the canvas to being a garbage piece of straight emotion, she took her temper, disgruntlement and maybe some fear locked inside her out on the canvas. Stroke after stroke, anger flowed from her fingertips.

Finally she changed colors and then again and again, and ended up with a soft cream color, which then turned to white, then sunshine yellow and followed by an amber. Finally, her chest heaving, her arm shaking, she stepped back to look at the garbage she'd thrown onto the canvas and froze. "What did I just create?"

She'd done this many times in her life, just thrown paint on a canvas with no expectation of a final product to share or to sell. It was just an outlet. The same as a lot of people who played golf or worked out in a gym. But she couldn't make heads or tails of what was in front of her.

Maybe that was because, all of a sudden, she was not making heads or tails of her own life.

And it had to do with this gallery show. Not only did it bother her, it *really* bothered her. But she couldn't begin to understand why. She neared the two canvases along the wall, one finished and one almost finished. Crouching down in front of them, she studied them. "They are both still nice," she said. "I just don't know if they are nice enough."

She straightened, realizing how tired she was. She glanced down at herself and winced. She'd forgotten to put on her painting smock. With a groan she walked out of her studio, closed and locked the door behind her and headed to her room. There was only a short hall in this section, and the whole area was her own personal space. Which was why she'd felt so odd when two of her guests had come up here. She should look at putting a door down below to seal off the third-floor stairway access. That would at least stop anybody from assuming the staircase was public.

Her guests had the run of the main floor, which was the living room/dining room/kitchen. The kitchen was still hers obviously. She didn't know how other bed-and-breakfast people ran their business, but it was something that Morning had taken a look at a few years back when she was interested in opening her own space. Because what she still needed was privacy. If she was upset or uneasy, she couldn't focus on painting something that was full of light and pleasure and sunshine. Her paintings would come out dark and aggressive and pure ugly.

She wandered back down the staircase, considering a door right at the entranceway. She had a little bit of money squirreled away for repairs because she had to keep her asset in good condition; otherwise, nobody would want to stay there. This stairway went right beside the kitchen, and she knew it was odd for a house to have more than one staircase, but it did happen, and it made sense with this new annex that her father and she had put on years ago.

When he came to visit, he stayed in one of the downstairs rooms below her sitting room. She never rented it out because it was his space. But he hadn't been here in a couple years. Neither had she been so overbooked that she had needed his space. She imagined she could certainly open it up and use it, if need be. It was hard to justify not doing so.

She walked into her father's rooms, turning on the light. Her glance swept through the space until she got to the large king bed in the center. And she frowned at a teddy bear on the bed.

"What the heck?" She walked closer. "No, not a teddy bear," she exclaimed. She picked up the gray mouse sitting on the bed. She didn't have a clue what it was or how it got here, and surely it hadn't been here when she was here last. When was that? She turned to look around the room. "I've got to be imagining this."

Just then her cell phone rang. It was Nancy. "Do you want to go for coffee somewhere? I'm bored."

And that was one of the big differences between Nancy and Morning. Morning was a morning person. At this time of day, she was almost ready to go to bed. She would have already had a bath and be tucked in with a good book, except she'd been so restless. And now she stood in her father's room, looking at something she didn't understand.

"Hey, you there?" Nancy asked.

"Yeah, I'm here. No, I can't go for coffee. It's been a long day," she said, and she certainly wasn't lying. "I wanted to paint more, but I've lost the light. And now I'm standing in my father's room, wondering how a stuffed mouse got onto his bed."

"That's easy, silly. Somebody put it there." Nancy laughed.

"Sure, but there haven't been any children here for a while."

"You said you had a family there a couple weeks ago."

"Yes, but they didn't come in here." She put the mouse back on the bed for the moment.

"I've told you how that's the problem with having people in your house. You have no idea where they go and when they go there," Nancy chided. "For all you know, they were playing in there the whole time."

"It's something to think about," Morning said. "I'd feel a whole lot better if it was just kids playing, but I certainly don't want to think of anything else having been on my father's bed."

Nancy's laughter pealed through the phone.

Morning stared down at the phone in her hand, more unnerved than she thought. Any other day she would have assumed exactly as Nancy had, that somebody had left it behind after playing in here, but right now she just wasn't so sure. It sat on the bed so perfectly. It could have been a parent thinking their child had gotten into the room accidentally and played with it and then tried to set things back to rights again. The trouble was, there were all kinds of possibilities, and none of them were good ones.

"Come on. Whatever is bothering you, let's go have a cup of coffee," Nancy said in a wheedling tone.

"It's pretty late for coffee," Morning said.

"Okay, so let's get you a hot milk then," Nancy cried in exasperation. "The walls are closing in on me. I just want to get out."

Making a sudden decision, Morning agreed. "Okay, but just for an hour. Curfew is for me too."

At that, Nancy laughed again. "It's your house. You can come in whenever."

Agreeing to meet in ten minutes, Morning snatched up the stuffed animal again and walked out. As she left, she took one last look at the room, realizing that nothing else appeared to be disturbed. She shrugged and closed the door, this time making sure she'd locked it. She had a lot of keys on her house ring. But the ones that never went anywhere were the ones for her own space and for her father's suite.

That room also had a sitting area and a full bathroom, plus it had a patio extending into the backyard. It was directly below her room, so she didn't think anybody could have been in there without her knowing. But then she wasn't always in her own rooms. She was often in the office working late, visiting with clients who had come in from out of town, old friends.

After placing the stuffed mouse in the hall closet, she walked to the front door, put on her sneakers and grabbed a hoodie. It wasn't cold out, but there was a chill inside her now. She walked out the door and closed it behind her, seeing Nancy across the road waiting for her. Morning waved. Now if only she knew how the hell that stuffed animal had gotten in her house and why.

GEIR AND JAGER sat in the vehicle outside the house. "Suggestions?" Geir asked.

"Anonymous tip?"

"And the footsteps?"

"Our imagination?"

They'd been through this since they'd gone downstairs and walked the entire house, finding no one. "I don't believe in ghosts," Geir said quietly.

"Neither do I," Jager said. "At least not the kind that can leave footprints."

"So, we missed him?"

"That would make sense, but the reason he was there doesn't mean it had anything to do with us."

Geir agreed. "Do you want to go back in?"

"I don't think so. Although we didn't check for ID on the body."

"He wasn't wearing anything."

"No, but, along with the bedding, his clothing was somewhere. Maybe stashed in the night table."

Geir looked at him. "So go in again?"

Jager frowned. "The more times we go in, the more danger there is we'll get caught and face a murder rap."

"I know. But the footsteps stopped us from doing a proper job."

"Okay, but five minutes only. Straight up to the bedroom, figure this out, if we can, and then leave."

Agreeing, they got out of the vehicle, walked around the block and retraced the route they had taken the first time. They also hadn't shut the window. As they hopped in through the window, Geir said, "That could be how our intruder got in."

Jager nodded. "We did give him an opening."

Back inside, they did a quick sweep on the main floor, then walked up to the master bedroom. Inside that room, they stepped forward with their flashlights on and searched the night tables and bedding. All they wanted to know was who this man was instead of waiting until the police or the media got a hold of the information.

"Well, this is interesting," Jager said from the far side of the bed.

Geir looked up. Just enough light shone through the window that he could see Jager's hands. "Is that a wallet?"

"The night table on this side is empty." Geir walked around to Jager's side, holding the flashlight so they could both see. They quickly took a look at the wallet.

"Wonder if this belongs to our dead guy here?"

"Maybe. Let's take photographs of what we find and get the hell out of here."

As Geir went to put the wallet back, Jager pulled out another one from the far back corner of the drawer to the nightstand. He opened it up. "Look at this."

They both froze. It was Mouse's ID under his birth name of O'Connor. "What year was the driver's license issued?"

"Five years ago."

They studied the picture.

Geir asked, "Why would his wallet be here?"

"Either he didn't need it anymore, or it was taken from him," Jager said in a hard tone.

They laid everything out on the bed, but the wallet held only money and a couple credit cards. They took photographs of it all and put it back in the wallet before returning it to the drawer.

As Geir went to close the drawer, he said, "It feels wrong to leave Mouse's wallet."

"Gotta leave it. Maybe it will trigger an investigation into this mess."

Hating to leave a piece of his friend here, Geir nonetheless agreed. "We need to be as official as we can but not be caught."

With one last look at the dead man, they headed to the stairs. Once again, they heard footsteps. With a finger to his lips, Jager slid down the banister so as to avoid making any noises on the stairs. He landed so softly on the main floor that there wasn't a sound. Geir went down behind him. Jager went left; Geir went right. They searched the floor, but nobody was here. Geir raced to the nearest window. "Shit." He pointed at somebody scrambling over the back fence.

"He's fast," Jager commented.

"Was he alone?" Moving silently, they swept through both floors of the house again and didn't find anything new. One after the other, they climbed out the window and closed it behind them. Instead of heading back to the truck, they followed the intruder's path around the house and out to the main road.

Up ahead, somebody talked on a cell phone, pacing nervously back and forth.

"Somebody was in the house, I tell you," Geir said, his voice hard.

Geir and Jager melted into the trees, grateful for a little cover. They stayed as close as they could, listening in. Geir remembered belatedly to pull out his phone and start the audio recording.

"Look. I told you. I saw somebody go in. Two somebodies. ... No, I don't know who they were," the man yelled. "It's your house. You come check it out. Hell, no, I'm not going back in there. There's a dead guy, remember?" He paced again, listening. "You owe me for this," he snapped. The conversation continued with interspersed silences where the young man paced back and forth.

Geir studied him carefully, but nothing was easily distinguishable. He wore jeans and a black hoodie, the hood over his head, like so many other people in the area. Geir watched and waited until the man hung up in frustration, but he continued to pace as if waiting. Geir and Jager waited quietly too. This was a game they well knew.

Fifteen minutes later an old Buick drove up, and the kid got in the front seat, snapping, "About time you got here. Did you bring the money?"

Beside him, Jager read off what he could see of the license plate into the audio. The plate was partially covered with mud—whether on purpose or not. They also couldn't see much of the driver. When the light had gone on as the young man had hopped into the front seat, still wearing his hoodie, they'd seen a beard and long hair on the driver, but that was it, not enough to identify either men. Whoever was in the vehicle drove away slowly. Geir and Jager slid out from their tree cover and walked down the sidewalk, keeping an eye on the vehicle. Up ahead it took a right and went around the corner. They were almost at the corner themselves. The vehicle had been driving that slowly.

An empty lot was beside them. On a sudden move, Geir bolted to the right, Jager following, ran through the lot, jumped the fence and raced out to the sidewalk. The vehicle had turned the corner and was slowly passing the teacher's house. When it pulled into the driveway and parked, Geir and Jager snuck down beside a nearby parked vehicle and watched.

The young guy with the hoodie yelled, "I don't want to go back in there."

"We have to check it out," the other man said, his voice calm, unflustered.

But the young man was not having anything to do with it. "You go in. You check it out."

"Sure, no problem, but you're the one who'll be seen hanging around." The older man slipped into the front door and left it slightly open. The young man looked around, paced back and forth, and then swore. He bolted inside.

Jager and Geir exchanged hard looks, ran up to the vehicle, confirming the license plate. The doors were closed on the vehicle but not locked.

With Jager opening a car door and checking the registration from the glove box, Geir slid toward the front door to the house and stood where he could hear the two inside. The door itself was still open, the young man needing a quick exit just in case.

From inside the house, Geir heard the young man once

again snapping, "Why are we here?"

Geir heard a *pop* sound, and his heart froze. The *pop* was followed by a slumping noise. Geir bolted around the garage, hiding from view.

Jager saw his actions, closed the vehicle door quietly and joined him. "What happened?" he whispered against Geir's ear.

"Sounded like a shot and a body hitting the floor."

Jager swore and pulled out his phone, slid over to the tree line on the far side of the property close to the neighbor's. Geir watched him disappear and realized he was putting in an anonymous tip to the police. Geir wondered how long it would take for somebody to arrive in this part of town. He joined Jager, where they could keep an eye on the comings and goings of the property.

Jager pointed to Geir's truck parked down a block. "Do you want to move it?"

Geir frowned. "Not sure we need to."

Jager nodded. "I suggest we sit and wait."

"What if he comes out and runs, disappears?"

"That would be good because then we could follow him. From here, we won't make it to the vehicle in time."

Geir nodded. "Gotcha."

And the two of them headed to Geir's truck. There they could watch and wait, in case this asshole tried to disappear.

CHAPTER 7

MORNING WALKED INTO the coffee shop and ordered an herbal tea. Nancy wasn't having anything to do with that. She ordered a thick black coffee. The two women took their drinks to a window seat and sat comfortably. Even for the lateness of the hour, the place was quite busy.

Nancy looked at Morning and said, "So tell me more about these men."

Morning sighed. "Is that the reason you wanted to meet? So you could get more details on them? You could have just done this on the phone."

"Well, they are staying with you, right?"

Morning nodded. "But they're here on business. And I don't know what kind of business," she answered, knowing the question she knew Nancy would ask next.

"And of course the idea is, it's none of your business, right?"

Morning chuckled. "That's right. They have a bed to sleep in and breakfast if they want it."

"You know? Maybe I should get into that business, considering the clientele you're attracting."

Morning smirked, shaking her head. "It's not like it's something I get a chance to do. I mean, determine who is staying there. Yes, I have the ultimate say on who it is, but I didn't know these men until they arrived."

"That's both exciting and scary," Nancy said.

"Maybe or maybe not." As she stared out the window, she thought she saw Geir's truck ripping past the coffee shop. She started and peered through the window. "Did you see that truck?"

"Yeah. I think they forgot the speed zones here," Nancy said in a drawled-out tone. "But then again they were going the same speed as that bloody car ahead of them."

Morning looked at her. "I didn't see the car."

Nancy shrugged. "I did. It looked like the truck was chasing the car. Or they were street racing," she added.

"I don't think they were racing." But, at the same time, Morning couldn't quite figure out if that had been Geir or not. Frowning, she stirred her herbal tea, wondering if the men were going home. If so, why so fast? It was only a block or so away.

"So, did you figure out that mouse thing?"

Morning shook her head. "No, but it's a little unsettling."

"Good. Maybe it'll make you more aware of your crazy clientele. And don't you normally keep that room locked?"

Morning raised her glance from the tea to her friend and nodded. "Yes, and it was unlocked when I went in."

"So, you know yourself how tired you can be after a painting session. So you forgot this time. No biggie." Nancy sat back, lifted her coffee and took a sip. "Man, I love this coffee."

Morning shook her head. "I still don't think it could have been kids. It was placed too specifically."

"Like I said, a mom trying to put things back together again, the way they belong."

Morning wasn't terribly happy with that concept because it meant two people had been in the room.

"Besides, your dad never stays there anyway, does he?"

Morning shook her head. "No, he never does."

"Is he still bugging you to sell the place?"

"Yes, but I haven't heard from him in a month."

"He's probably just giving you a chance to get used to the idea, and then he'll hit you up even harder."

"Maybe."

"How's the painting going?"

On a bright note Morning felt her spirits rise as she shared what was going on with her studio and her upcoming showing.

"That sounds fantastic," Nancy said, leaning forward. "When do I get to see them?"

Morning shook her head. "Not before Friday. I'll take them down and show the gallery owner. Hopefully he'll feel justified in giving me the chance."

"Self-confidence, remember? You need to have more faith in what you do."

"Sure, but what I was doing was just pretty pictures. This is something more," she confessed. "And I want to do more. I want to do a lot of *more*."

"And the bed-and-breakfast gives you that option," Nancy said. "You're doing way better with that than I am with my teaching. I can't get a job anywhere."

"And yet the teachers and the principals all tell you to give it time, to do your substitute days wherever they put you, and eventually you'll get a full-time job."

"That's what they say, but ..." Nancy's voice trailed off, obviously depressed at the thought for the moment.

"And didn't you say you were still looking at moving?"

"Well, there's something I didn't tell you. My mom was

talking about moving back home again. When I talked to her yesterday morning, she said she and Dad were maybe done with traveling."

"You'll be happy to see them."

"Yes, but not happy to give up the house I have enjoyed entirely alone," she said with a drawn smile. "It's nice to have independence."

Morning smiled in understanding. "I know, but we're both tied to our parents in some ways. If my dad forces the issue, then, in theory, I have to sell. There's no way I can afford to buy him out. Not with property prices what they are these days."

"I know. I feel the same way. So, yeah, I was thinking about moving. I just don't have a location."

"True, but you've talked about various places over the years, from Washington State to Texas to Maine." She laughed. "You have a lot more states to choose from."

Nancy shrugged. "And yet nothing appeals. I want to move. I want independence. But I want a job."

"Have you been applying?"

Nancy smiled. "Now here's the surprise," she said. "I *have* been applying. I sent out three different résumés yesterday after we talked."

"Excellent." At the same time Morning felt a pain in her chest. "As much as I want you to be happy, I'll miss you."

Nancy leaned forward. "Well, since we're talking about fictional jobs and fictional moves, why don't you join me? You can sell this place to get your father off your back. You'll end up with a very decent chunk of money to live somewhere else, to buy yourself a house. It would give you time for your painting."

Morning sighed. "I'm a long way from being able to live

off my paintings, but it's a nice thought."

"But you don't know that. You can buy another bed-and-breakfast, have no mortgage, have no father breathing down your back and still be independent, doing what you want to do."

"I'll think about it, but, like you said, it's a fictional location." She gave a little laugh and glanced at her watch. "It's a quarter to eleven. I need to go home."

The two women stood. Outside the coffeehouse, they stopped for a moment, then walked down the block. As they got closer to their houses, Morning saw lights on in her bed-and-breakfast. "Somebody's home," she said. "Considering curfew is up anytime now, that's a good thing."

"It's still creepy. Strangers in your space."

Morning chuckled. "I prefer to think of them as friends I haven't met."

"Only if they're nice people. A lot of weirdos are out there."

Morning looked up and thought she saw a shadow cross one of the bedroom windows.

As they got closer, Nancy said, "Which one of the sexy guys is in that room?"

Morning checked the other lights. "I don't know. One is in that room, and the other is on the same side but at the back of the house." But, as she could see, the light was on in the front. But she swore it hadn't been on when she had left.

"HE JUST TOOK a left."

Geir yelled, "I see him." He quickly turned the vehicle left, then took a right, changed lanes and followed the car.

"Any idea where he's going?" Jager asked.

"He's trying to shake us off his tail."

"And it looks like he's looping back around again."

"Shit," Geir said as he wrenched the rear tire on a hard-right corner, tires squealing. "The cops should've had him. We called a long time ago."

"We don't know what might have delayed the cops," Jager said. He held on to the dash and to the seat belt across his chest. "Is it my imagination, or is he working his way back toward the bed-and-breakfast again?"

"Bastard. I bet he is," Geir snapped. "Morning is too nice, too friendly and too open. An asshole like that could take advantage of her."

"I know. But she's one of those sunshine kind of people who sees the good in everyone. And we've been in the shadows for so long that we don't know anything other than the darker side."

"Which is why Morning is special," Geir said, his lips twitching. "I don't understand who she is and how she can be like she is."

"She's never had to deal with a negative dark side or the scary side, like we have."

Sure enough, three corners later, they were ripping down the same street they'd been up before. Only this time, up ahead, standing on the sidewalk talking, were two women. "Oh, please no," Geir yelled.

The Buick in front of them turned and veered right toward the women.

Geir hit his horn hard, and the girls jumped out of the way as the lead vehicle bounced up the curb, missed them, bounced back onto the street again and tore off into the night.

Geir pulled up beside the women, and both men raced out of the truck. Geir ran toward Morning Blossom, who was sitting in shock on the grass. He crouched beside her. "Are you okay?"

She stared up at him with a glazed look. "Did that car just try to run us down?"

His hands were busy checking out her hips and legs as he nodded.

"Really?" She looked at him. "What about Nancy? Is she hurt?"

"No, she's fine." Geir had already seen Jager help her to her feet. Geir glanced at her. "I asked if you were okay, and you didn't answer me."

She sighed. "Give me a hand up."

He helped her to her feet, and she winced.

She stood on one foot, her other lifted off the grass.

"Did you twist your ankle?"

"Maybe, I don't know." She tried to put her weight on her foot and swore gently as she brought it back up again. "Looks like it. Crap. I can't afford this. I need my feet. My house has a lot of stairs."

Without any warning he bent, scooped her into his arms and carried her inside the B&B.

She laughed and protested. "I can walk, you know."

"Hardly." He carried her into the kitchen, put her in a chair with her feet up on the chair beside her, where he gently eased her injured foot out of its shoe. "I'll get some ice on that right away."

"It's not that bad. I can at least put my weight on it now. It hurts, but it's not terrible."

"And, if we get it treated right away, it'll be that much easier." He came back from the freezer with a bag of frozen peas.

She raised her eyes. "Well, those were for your dinner tomorrow night."

He chuckled. "Maybe not." He walked into the living room, grabbed a cushion off one of the couches and returned, putting it under her foot. He looked back at her. "Are you feeling in shock at all?" His gaze was intent on her cheeks and her eyes. Her eyes were still dilated slightly, but she didn't appear to be further injured.

She shook her head. "Honest, I'm fine. It was just such a surprise to have that car come up onto the sidewalk."

"Even worse, I'm afraid it was intended."

She stared at him wordlessly, her jaw dropping. "It wasn't an accident? He wasn't just trying to catch a cell phone on the floor or something and twisted the wheel accidentally?"

Geir shook his head. "I don't think so. We'd been chasing him for the last ten minutes. This was the second time he'd come up this street. I'm afraid it was on purpose."

She stared at him. "So did they know it was me, or was he just trying to run anyone down so you would stop and help us?"

He sat back and looked at her. "That's a good question. I don't have an answer for you."

"Why were you chasing him?"

"Because we think he shot somebody when we were standing outside a house."

This time her eyes grew round, and she stared at him. "Wow. Your life is exciting."

He chuckled. "Some excitement I could do without."

"No doubt," she muttered. "It's past curfew now. I wonder if everybody is in."

"What do you normally do at curfew?"

"I lock all the doors. If guests haven't made it back, they haven't made it back."

He nodded. "In that case I'll do that."

Jager stood in the doorway between the kitchen and living room. "No, I can do it. You stay here."

Morning turned to look at him. "How is Nancy?"

"She's fine. She was farther back than you were from the street."

"Oh, good. I'd feel terrible if she had been hit."

"I walked her home to make sure she was okay, but she's fine. I also called in the hit and run and passed on the license plate info. Who knows if we'll hear anything back."

"Good. And I'm sure Nancy loved that," Morning said in a dry tone. "She thinks you two are cute and sexy."

"That's because we are," Geir said with a grin.

Jager disappeared rather than answering.

She looked back at Geir. "He needs to know where all the keys are."

Geir frowned at her. "You need keys to lock up?"

"Just this back kitchen door." She hesitated.

"Where are the keys?"

She reached into her pocket and pulled out her key ring with at least a dozen keys on it. She fished out the right one and handed it to him. "This will lock the kitchen door here. The front door has a bolt."

"And we have to check the French doors."

When Jager returned to the kitchen, Geir handed Jager the keys. "You can lock that kitchen door right there."

After he did so, the keys were returned to Morning. They lifted the ice pack and took a closer look. "We'll do this off and on for the next hour. Ten minutes or so at a time to make sure the swelling doesn't get too bad. Then you need to stay off it as much as you can."

"Well, I can stay off it for a little while," she said, "but honestly it wasn't that bad. I think it's just twisted from being tossed off my feet. I wrenched it slightly."

"Maybe, but you still need to be off it as much as you can be."

And true to their word they sat there for the next hour and did ice packs off and on until she protested. "Okay, that's enough. I've got to go to bed."

Geir nodded, bent forward, eyeing her foot, and said, "Try standing."

She got on her feet and took a tentative step. "It's not that bad."

"But not that good."

She shrugged. "I can walk on it." And she took several short steps.

Geir could see the pain cross her face, but it didn't appear to be all that bad. "Come on. Let me help you upstairs." He placed an arm around her shoulders. Together they traveled to the bottom of the stairs, then he helped her up to her room. Once there, he smiled and said, "Good night." A few feet away he turned to see her standing at the doorway, staring at him. "Anything wrong?"

She flushed. "No, everything's fine," she said as she closed the door.

CHAPTER 8

O N THURSDAY, SHE woke to the early morning call of birds outside her window. She hadn't had a great night, tossing and turning, wondering at what kind of a fool she was that she'd stood staring after Geir at the doorway. She put it down to shock, but, at the same time, she knew it was a lot more than that. She flung back the bedcovers and sat up. Her ankle was swollen slightly, but it wasn't too bad, considering.

She got on her feet experimentally and walked slowly to the bathroom. The foot was functional, but the guys were right; she should stay off it as much as possible. She had an ace bandage that she wrapped around it for support. Then she did a quick wash up, got dressed, and, hopping on her good foot, she went down the back staircase to the kitchen. In the kitchen she put on coffee and thought about what she needed to do for breakfast. At the moment, she wasn't feeling like putting in a grand effort.

But everybody had come to expect a certain level of food. She decided cream scones were fast and easy. She whipped up a batch and tossed them in the oven. She was afraid to sit down because she'd never want to get back up again. At the same time, if a task could be done sitting down, all the better.

She poured herself a cup of coffee, sitting, her foot on

the pillow left from the night before, with the online edition of her local morning paper pulled up on her laptop, and perused the headlines. There was the usual mayhem going on in the world. She hated the crazy politics, the wars, and the whole confusion and backstabbing mess in politics. She shut her laptop and sipped her coffee.

Hearing a bright whistle coming in behind her, she spoke without looking behind her, "Good morning, Geir."

"How did you know it was me?" he asked lightly as he walked toward the counter with the coffeepot, got a cup from the cabinet and poured himself a cup.

"Your voice is easy to distinguish," she said with a smile.

"Interesting. Well, since you already know who I am, and you already recognize my voice, then we're past being strangers now, aren't we?"

She stared at him suspiciously. "We're not exactly friends either."

His eyes widened. "I'm hurt. I thought we were much closer than friends."

She shook her head at his teasing tone. "I know guys like you. They dash into town and cause trouble, then disappear just as fast."

"As long as we cause fun while we're in town, and everybody is enjoying life, and nobody gets hurt ..."

"True enough, but I'm not one of those women who'll be part of your drop-into-town-and-have-fun saga."

"Nope, you're a forever kind of girl."

She lifted her coffee cup and stared at him over the rim. "What do you mean by that?"

"It means, you're not a one-night-stand kind of girl. When you let somebody into your bed, it's because it's something you want long term. It takes a lot for you to trust, and, when you do, you trust deeply."

"People would say the opposite about me because I have a bed-and-breakfast. That I'm too trusting to let people into my home. Therefore, I trust easily."

He studied her. "I think that's the business side of you. I think you're an extrovert and enjoy having people around. But, to let them into your inner world, I think that takes a lot of trust."

She could feel heat crawling up her neck. "That's very astute of you." She hurriedly stood. As soon as she did, she winced, and he was at her side.

"Hey, remember? You need to stay off that foot. You've done enough just getting from the third floor to the first floor. How is the ankle this morning?"

"Fine, I just stepped wrong or too fast." She motioned toward the stove. "I have scones in the oven. I need to take them out."

"You sit down. I'll take care of them." He grabbed an oven mitt and opened the door. Instantly the smell of cream scones filled the kitchen. He pulled out the cookie sheet and took them to her. "Do they look done to you?"

She eyed the golden tops with just the barest rim of a darker golden color on the base and nodded. "They're perfect."

He put them on top of the stove, closed the oven door and turned the temperature knob to Off. He looked around. "Where are your racks?"

"In that drawer."

He pulled out a rack and placed it on the center island and deftly transferred the scones to it. He put the cookie sheet by the sink and brought the coffeepot to her, filling her cup. "So we didn't get much of a chance to see each other last evening. How did your evening go?"

She wanted the small talk. "It was fine. Other than realizing that previous guests had gotten into my father's rooms when I hadn't been watching and not being able to paint because I had no natural light and being too unsettled to sit down with a good book—but, otherwise, it was fine."

He stared at her for a moment. "Somebody was in rooms you don't allow people in?"

She shrugged. "My father has the set of rooms below mine. His sitting room, bathroom and bedroom were part of the annex out back. He owns half of this house."

"And somebody was in there?" he prompted.

She shrugged. "Well, kids, at least. I found a stuffed animal on the bed," she said with a smile. "The trouble was, it wasn't like it was tossed on the bed—disturbed, as if kids had been climbing all over the place—but more like it had been placed very deliberately atop the covers where the pillows are."

"What kind of a stuffed animal?"

She stared at him, her lips quirked. "A great big gray mouse." She watched as a stillness came over him.

He slowly raised his eyes to look at her intently. "A mouse?"

She nodded. "A mouse with a big silly grin."

He raised his hands and put them about a foot apart and said, "A mouse about this size?"

She frowned, leaning forward. "Yes. How did you know?"

"A mouse with shiny eyes and a big goofy grin?"

She nodded slowly. "Is it yours?"

He shook his head slowly. "Would you mind showing it to me please?"

She shrugged. "I put it in the hall closet, and then I locked the door to my father's rooms."

He hopped to his feet and said in a low voice, "It's important."

"So much for staying off my feet," she muttered. But she led him to her father's rooms down the hall in the back addition. "The house is a bit of a maze because of the way we built the addition," she said by way of apology.

He didn't say a word, just stayed with her.

She walked to the hall closet and pulled out the mouse, passing it to him. Then led him to her father's door. She unlocked it and pushed it open. She walked to the bedroom door, opening it also. She motioned at the bed. "It was lying in the center at the pillows." She ignored the mouse in his arms, too interested in the change that overcame his features. There was a stillness, an alertness, an almost predatory look on his face. "What does it mean to you?"

He slowly shook his head as he examined the stuffed animal from all angles.

She hadn't considered there might be anything in it, but he was squeezing it as if thinking along that line.

Finally he lifted his head and said, "I'm not sure what it means or why it's here, but we found an identical one in a house we were at last night."

"The house where the guy was shot?"

He looked at her and nodded. "And where we found another dead body. We found the dead body first. Then the other man was shot afterward."

She shook her head. "What does a gray mouse have to do with murdered men?"

"The dead man was found in the master bedroom, but the mouse was found in the children's room. The room had been painted in bright cheerful colors, but it showed signs of age. Yet in the corner was a new stuffed mouse."

She stared straight at him. "Okay. Now that's bizarre."

"No, it's more than that," he said quietly.

"You can have the mouse," she said. "I sure as hell don't want it. Especially now that you're thinking those kinds of thoughts."

He turned and glanced at her. "I don't think it's the same mouse, ... just for clarity here."

She winced. "Neither do I. But now that you put that thought in my head ..."

He smiled. "No, it's definitely identical to the one I saw in that dilapidated old bedroom, just not the *same* one."

"How did the man in the master bedroom die?"

He turned, looked at her briefly, and said, "He was stabbed. The thing is, he died a few weeks ago. Who knows how long it would have been left there if we hadn't gone in."

Not a concept she wanted to contemplate.

"Let's put it back in the hall closet," he said quietly. "At least for the moment."

She shuddered but nodded. She locked up her father's rooms and pointed to where she'd stored the mouse earlier. As she closed the door, she asked, "Who lived in the house?"

"It was obviously deserted. We thought it might belong to one of the teachers at Midlands High School."

"Hang on a minute. I'm confused. You're saying this house—that had one murdered man in it and then another man was shot in it—belongs to one of the teachers who works at the same school where Nancy sometimes works?" Morning stared at Geir in bewilderment. "Who owns the house?"

"Well, we looked up the owner's name. We're not sure

he's a teacher at Midlands High School, but the owner name is a match for one of the teachers' names—not that there couldn't be more than one person with this particular name. And we're not 100 percent sure that he's the person we're looking for. The guy we need to find consistently uses a nickname, although his fake names seem to change."

"What nickname?"

"Poppy?"

Instantly she felt the color drain from her cheeks. "Poppy?"

He spun in a slow circle and looked at her. Then walked close to her, reaching out to grab her hands. "Do you know him?"

She stared up at him and nodded her head. "He was pretty famous way back when."

"Famous in what way?"

"Among the kids at school."

He shook his head. "Can you give me more information please?"

"He hung around with a young boy for years. A couple of them. There was lots of talk about him at the time, but I don't know how true any of it was."

"Did you know him personally?"

"Not really." She waved her hand. "Honestly I blocked most of it out."

"But this"—Geir waved his hand around her house—"isn't Poppy's kind of neighborhood."

She gave him a sad smile. "I didn't always live here. I used to live with my mom, but she was a junkie. That lifestyle was her undoing. She died about eight years ago. When I was seven, I came to live with my dad. That's when I moved in here."

He still held her hands, lifting one close to his lips and kissed it gently. "Where did your mom live?" When she recited her childhood street address, he sighed. "Is that the same street the guy you know as Poppy lived on?"

"Yes. I lived across the street from his house."

He nodded. "That was the house I was at last night."

"And a murdered man was in there? And it wasn't Poppy?"

"I don't know. We're waiting on the police for that. The house was registered to a Reginald Henderson."

She stared at him mutely. "Is it wrong of me to be happy if that's Poppy and that he's dead?" She knew she should just be quiet, but Poppy was not a name or an individual she wanted to remember.

"How well did you know Poppy?"

She shook her head. "I didn't know him very well at all. But we all knew about him. The kids all talked about him."

"None of the adults did anything?"

"Poppy was Poppy for a reason," she said drily. "He always had food, booze and drugs. Whatever you needed, Poppy would help you get it."

"So he kept the talk down by making the children happy so nobody reported him."

She shrugged. "I guess. I wasn't of an age to have anything to do with that. But I do remember a couple boys not wanting to play on the block because it was Poppy's block, and they didn't want to meet him. He was kind of creepy."

"We think that this Poppy might work at the school where Nancy was yesterday."

She stared at him in horror. "That's not good."

"Could you identify him from a current photo?"

"I don't know. It was a long time ago."

"Did he ever touch you?"

She shook her head. "Honestly I don't think he cared about girls. I think he was all about boys." She watched as Geir nodded.

"That would be Poppy."

"Do you have pictures of him?"

"We'd have to go to the school website and see if you recognize him."

She turned and hobbled her way back to the kitchen. "Then let me take a look at it."

Back in the kitchen, they sat at the table while he opened his laptop, then looked up the website with the staff directory for the school. "Take a look at these."

She looked at the full page of photos and slowly studied each one, scanning down to the next row and the next row. On the last row she paused, reaching out a finger, placing it on a picture. "I'd say that's him."

He came around and stood behind her. "Are you sure?"

She shrugged. "As much as a seven-year-old can remember, yes."

He nodded. "It's not conclusive evidence, but it's a big help."

"Why? Is that the man whose house you were at?"

He smiled and nodded. "Absolutely. Reginald Henderson is the registered owner of the house across the street from your childhood home. That's the house where we were at last night."

She stared at the photograph and felt her stomach heave. "I figured, when I left that life with my mom and came to live with my dad, well, I was grateful to leave all that behind. At the same time, I always felt guilty because I got out and nobody else did."

"You don't know that," he said quietly. "For all you know, other kids got out too."

She looked up at him. "Poppy wasn't always here, you know? He used to come and go to other places."

"Any idea where those other places were?"

She grimly smiled and nodded. "Texas, I think. He used to go to Texas."

GEIR LISTENED, HEARING the word *Texas* again. He nodded. "He was in Texas for quite a while."

She nodded again. "I think he was in a lot of places. But he had to have a reason for going from one state to the other."

"Maybe things got too hot here?" he suggested.

She shrugged. "I think I heard something about Washington State in there too."

Geir settled back. "Honestly I imagine a lot of states are involved."

"Well, if he's a pedophile and crossed state lines, can't you get the FBI's help?"

"I could if it was made official."

"If there were a lot of victims, I would think they'd need justice. Not to mention closure."

"Plus he needs to be stopped. He's *still* playing his games."

"If he's in his early sixties now, chances are good he has been doing this for forty-plus years."

"Yes. His brother committed suicide as a teen. So it could quite easily span forty to forty-five years, if his brother was a victim too."

"What sends a man onto that path? It's hard to think about."

He nodded. "How does anyone know? Maybe he was abused as a child too, not that I would feel sorry for him at this point because he took that abuse and turned it against everyone else."

She shuddered. "Well, at least the police have it now to handle."

He gave her a lopsided grin. "They do, and they don't."

She stared at him and sighed. "Meaning, you haven't shared all the information with them?"

"We did make an anonymous phone call so the two bodies from last night would be found. As we learn more over the next couple days, we can come forward with it all and approach the police but only to a handpicked officer chosen by Mason."

"I wonder how long that poor man lay there."

"It's hard to say, but the man who was later shot knew about the dead body. I heard that much."

"So he was shot to keep him quiet?"

"As far as we can figure."

She got up and poured coffee for both of them. "So what do you do now?"

"Continue our research. If it was Poppy who shot this most recent guy last night, we did get the registration and license plate off the car he drove."

"The car you were chasing?"

"Yes."

She shook her head. "I need to be in my studio as much as I can. I must have several paintings ready for tomorrow."

"Are you worried about it?"

"Yes. I think the gallery owner is hesitant about letting

me have a spot. He's very protective about the work hitting his quality level. And I'm very concerned about hitting it too." She gave Geir a wry smile.

He nodded. "In that case, I hope you'll have a good day painting."

She nodded. "I think I also have one couple leaving today. And I'm not sure about Ken, the other gentleman."

"I haven't seen him yet." Geir frowned. "I haven't met the couple either."

She chuckled. "They might be honeymooners," she said. "Besides, not everyone is up at the crack of dawn, like I am."

He grinned. "There are worse ways to spend the time."

"In a lot of ways, there's nothing better, if it's with somebody you care about."

He flashed her a bright smile. "Not into these current dating apps, hook-up apps?"

She shook her head and shuddered. "No. Nancy was explaining how, on an app she's familiar with, everyone has casual sex, but kissing is considered too intimate and to be saved for lovers. How messed up is that? That is definitely not my style."

"It certainly appears to be working for a lot of people." Although privately he agreed with her, he couldn't think of anything worse.

Just then Jager came in the kitchen. "Time to go."

Something in his voice had Geir nodding agreeably. He stood, smiled at Morning and said, "See? We're progressing nicely. We've already decided we don't like dating apps, prefer kissing on a first date to having sex without thought or a connection. And both of us think you should go to the studio and have a great day." He tossed her shocked face a bright smile and disappeared behind Jager.

He knew he'd shocked her. It wasn't exactly hard to imagine what that look on her face meant. And he was okay with that. She was a sweetheart and way too trusting. But she was also fun to tease. He'd seen the color wash up her cheeks at his words. But now she'd have a chance to either cool off or calm down.

Jager shot him a look as they walked out the front door. "What was that all about?"

Geir chuckled. "We were discussing the merits or lack of merits of some of the dating apps and how society today is apparently okay with having sex but not kissing first or dating."

Jager stopped and gave him a long look. "What?"

Geir patted him on the shoulder. "See? We're just too old for this shit."

Jager shook his head. "Speak for yourself. But I can't say I'd want to skip on the kissing part. I really like kissing."

"You and me both."

As they headed to Geir's truck, Geir turned to him. "Did the police ever make it to our double-homicide crime scene?"

Jager nodded. "I picked up chatter about it on the police band."

"Where are we going now?"

"Levi found a second property under Poppy's name. It was under both names but was transferred to Poppy several years ago."

"Mouse owned the house?"

"Both his and Poppy's names were on the title originally. As if they were family or business partners."

Geir stared at Jager, and his stomach twisted in a crazy knot. "Are we thinking they might be related?"

"It would certainly explain how Poppy got close to Mouse. I doubt they shared a blood relationship, but *family* is a loose term in Mouse's life, given his mother's continuous stream of boyfriends, don't forget. It would certainly explain how Poppy stayed close to Mouse. Opportunity is so much of the problem for these pedophiles, particularly if they're not looking for a quick flash and then a death to the relationship. They want somebody to groom and to be close to them all the time."

"That's just sick," Geir said. He turned the key in the engine, pulling out into traffic. "So where is this second property?"

"Not very far away from the other property. Only about six blocks from where we were last night. On the more affluent side of life."

"Poppy living on the *better side of life?*" Geir shook his head. "Is it just me, or is that some sick bastard who would do that to his own kin?"

"The question is what kin? We never could find any family related to Mouse."

"I hate that we still don't have enough information to figure this out," Geir said.

"I know. But we're getting there. Did you notice anything different about Morning?"

Geir took a corner that would lead him down the block to the house they'd been at last night, figuring that at least he'd go past that area before heading to the new location. He glanced at Jager and asked, "In what way?"

"Did you see how many times she looked out the window?"

"Looking for someone? Waiting for someone?" He told Jager about the stuffed mouse she'd found. "She's got no idea how it got into her place."

"She was almost struck by a hit-and-run driver. An intruder, a stupid stuffed mouse, ... that's an awful lot of circumstantial bits and pieces but nothing conclusive."

As they approached Poppy's first house, they saw the cops were still outside, and crime scene tape had been wrapped around the yard. Geir nodded with satisfaction. "Good. At least they're still working here."

He drove down the block, took the corners as per Jager's instructions, pulled up beside a small brick rancher and parked just past it. Before he got out of the vehicle, he called Morning. When she answered, slightly breathless, he said, "Are you okay?" His voice was sharper than he'd intended.

There was an odd silence for a moment; then she said, "Yes, of course. Why wouldn't I be?"

"Because you're out of breath, as if you were running."

"I was going upstairs to my studio. It still takes effort with my ankle." She laughed. "Why are you calling?"

"Jager brought up an interesting fact, and I hate to say it, but I didn't notice because I was so focused on our conversation and on you," he said in a light tone. "You kept looking out the windows, but it wasn't a nice look-see, rather as if you're worried. Have you had any intruders, any strangers in the backyard that I don't know about?"

Silence.

He closed his eyes and pinched the bridge of his nose. "When and how often?"

"Look. It was nothing. I just saw somebody in the backyard yesterday, that's all."

"What was he doing, and where was he?" He exchanged a cold glance with Jager.

"He was running away from the house toward the back

fence, and he bolted over it at the corner."

"Can you give me any identifying points?"

"No, just very tall and wiry."

He sighed. "When?"

"It's not like this was a crime or anything, and I'm not in trouble for not telling you," she snapped. Immediately she sighed. "I'm sorry. I don't mean to be rude. I know you're calling because you're worried about me."

"When?"

She sighed. "Yesterday. Then I found the mouse."

"Anything else?"

Reluctantly she said, "I thought I had locked the door to my studio, but, when I went up there yesterday, it was unlocked."

"Shit," he snapped. "I want the names of everybody staying there since we arrived because I presume that's the only time you've had these incidences?"

"Are you saying you brought them into my world?" She tried to keep her voice light.

"Don't evade the question."

"It wasn't a question. You gave an order. I'll look it up when you get home."

"You'll look it up now, so I can run the names through a friend of ours."

"But they're my guests," she cried out.

"And what if they're not? What if they've moved in because we're there?"

"And how would they know?"

"I don't know yet, but I have to consider all avenues. I have to make sure you're safe."

"Someone running in my backyard is not an issue. And it does happen, you know?"

"Yeah? When was the last time it happened?"

He could almost hear the wheels of her mind churning as she tried to come up with an answer.

"So long ago you can't remember."

"Okay, fine. So it's been a while. That doesn't mean a whole lot," she said in exasperation. "The man who is staying is Ken Wiley."

"Did you know him before?"

"No."

"And the couple?"

"They said they've been here before," she said. "Although not for a few years."

"Names?"

"Bruce and Brenda Carter," she said. "I believe they're from Texas."

"Do they ever use airport shuttles or buses to come in? Do they take taxicabs? How do they get to your place from the airport?"

"I don't know, and I don't care," she cried out. "Do you hear yourself? I don't investigate any of my guests. It's not part of what I do."

"I hear you, but maybe it's something you should be doing." With that he hung up, glanced at Jager, motioned to the house and said, "Let's go."

CHAPTER 9

MORNING STOOD IN the middle of her studio, her cell phone in her pocket, her face buried in her hands. To the empty room she said, "How am I supposed to paint in an environment like this?"

She needed peace and quiet. She needed the house to be silent. She needed to be in the right mood. If she painted in the wrong mood, it showed in her work. And it showed in an ugly way.

She walked gingerly to the French doors, testing her ankle, and stepped onto her small balcony. She tried to remember what the man had looked like as he ran away from the house. At the time, she figured somebody had walked around to the back of her house, maybe checking it out, then heard something and got scared. Obviously she didn't operate in the world Geir and Jager did. And it was distressing to think that, because of them, this scary element was coming into her world.

Though it had taken her weeks, if not months—okay, potentially years—she'd slowly cocooned into this home being her safe zone. After years of not feeling safe, after years of watching people come and go—her mother's friends, other drug addicts, alcoholics, and all the other things that went along with people who were involved in that industry—she'd needed a safe zone.

She'd taken to life with her father almost with a frenzied gratitude. And, when she'd realized she was finally safe, that this was a place where she could stay *forever*, she'd taken that to heart and had put down roots, building herself almost a cage instead of enjoying the freedom this life gives her. She shook her head. "Well, how absolutely stupid is that?"

But it was true because this was where she had nested the whole time. And from here she'd blossomed. In more ways than one, considering her name. But, as she'd learned to relax and had decided that no more strangers were coming into her house without her knowing about it, she realized just how much she'd taken to her life here. When she had broached the idea of turning it into a bed-and-breakfast, her father had looked at her in surprise, and she'd been smiling and happy, not even concerned about her childhood history.

Which showed how much growth she had gone through back then. But more recently, when the situation had been reversed, when her father had broached her about selling his half of the house, she had looked at him in utter surprise. And her childhood history had surfaced from the locked away place deep in her brain.

But now, as she considered the additional fear that came to mind with Geir's questions, she realized maybe it wasn't as much about her inner growth as much as it was that she'd taken all that history and had stomped it into a deep dark corner of her mind and had slammed the door shut on it all.

But she hadn't dealt with it. Because the minute something uncertain went on, it brought up that old fear again. Fear that her safety zone was being taken away. And that she couldn't tolerate.

Nancy had talked about how she might be moving, and, at the time, she'd spoken about Morning moving on too.

You could sell the house. It would fetch decent money. With your half, you could buy another house. Maybe have another bed-and-breakfast with no mortgage, particularly if you moved out of this very popular high-priced real estate area. But it had been a mere suggestion—not one Morning had seriously considered.

And she knew that, as soon as she did consider it seriously, that sense of safety inside her would feel ripped apart because it already was now. And yet seeing the man run across her backyard hadn't done it to her. Seeing the stuffed mouse on the bed in her father's room hadn't done it to her. Not even getting almost run down last night outside on her yard.

Not until Geir had asked her questions. … Only then was her safe world shaken, making her realize just how much of a fake bubble of happiness she'd been living in and how that bubble was so very necessary for her own peace of mind.

She was naturally optimistic—a fun, outgoing, breezy kind of person. But what was she supposed to do when it came to this nightmare the men were involved in? And she didn't even know all the details.

She leaned against the balcony railing and stared down, seeing the windows to her father's sitting room below her. His set of French doors were there as well, underneath her own. But he had a patio where she had the balcony. It would be much harder for an intruder to get up on the second floor, and yet it would be easy enough to get in the glass doors if they weren't locked. She reached up a shaky hand to her cheek and wondered, "Is that how the mouse got here?" Something was so very unsettling about an incongruent item like that in a space where it had no business being, to know that somehow it got there and not by her own hand. She'd been totally happy thinking that maybe a child had placed it there, until she remembered she hadn't had children staying at the house in a long time. And she knew, for a fact, that she'd been in her father's room about a week ago.

She turned and walked back inside her studio, wandering around, checking out her paintings. She stopped in front of the five nice *pretty* pictures and frowned. "You really are terrible, aren't you?"

She gingerly squatted in front of them, favoring her good ankle, her mind caught on the almost postcard look to them. She stood and wandered a little bit farther, where the new finished painting sat. She studied it for a long moment and smiled. "This is special." The second one sat on the floor beside the first, but the second painting was only half done.

She wandered around to the easel and stared at the angry red painting, the supposed throwaway canvas. It was an abstract with a weird luminescent glow of yellow through it. She stepped back from the painting, feeling it tug deep inside her. She shook her head. "Well, you're not what I expected." She studied it a moment longer. "Maybe that is a good thing."

She took the red painting onto the rear balcony into the natural light, and she propped it against the railing. Then she backed up against the house so she could see it in the sunlight but from a slight distance. The balcony was only three feet deep and eight feet long, so she didn't have a whole lot of room. But still it gave her an idea about how it would appear to somebody else looking at it. There was a magnetic pull about it. She'd certainly painted it with passion, and it was almost as if that same passion sucked her into the canvas now.

She shook her head. "You're just getting fanciful." She

brought it back inside and set it down beside the newly finished ones, picked up the almost-finished one and placed it on the easel. She grabbed her smock. If she didn't muck up this painting, this one could be number two.

With her head bent, she returned to work, delicately picking up the last bits of trim needed for the buildings before gathering the foggy colors moving over the cityscape in waves. Then she went about highlighting the accented yellow and orange from the sunrise that crept through the center. Something was very disturbing about the image—but in a good way. She had to admit she was happy with that. She left the painting on the easel as she turned for a rag, cleaned up her brushes, and then, realizing what time it was, headed back downstairs. She took her time, not wanting to move too fast and reinjure her ankle.

She hadn't gone to her studio until the breakfast hours for her guests were done. But she wondered about them, as she hadn't seen the other guests. She often had people who didn't want breakfast. Either the breakfast was so far off their own diet that they had to abstain or they were heading to town to enjoy what else could be offered. And Morning certainly appreciated both cases. It was almost lunchtime now. She shook her head. "Where did the morning go?"

Just then her phone rang. She smiled when she saw it was Nancy. Morning put her cell phone on the kitchen counter, pushing the Speaker icon. She picked up a knife, grabbing a purple onion off the island, already creating a salad. "Nancy, what's up?"

"Just checking to make sure you were okay after last night."

"I'm fine. The ankle is still wrapped, but it's not bad."

"Are you sure you should be on it?"

"It's fine," Morning said quietly. "What about you? Did you sleep?"

"Well, I was quite prepared to let Jager have a closer look at me, to make sure everything was all right, but he didn't seem interested." Nancy's voice was wreathed in regret.

Morning chuckled. "He's not the kind of guy you play around with lightly."

"Are you kidding? He looks like the kind of guy who's a moth to a flame. You'll either fly high and enjoy the heat or you'll burn to a crisp. I just thought, maybe for once, I could be a moth to the flame and find out what real passion is like."

Morning stared out the window. "You've had lots of passion in your life."

"Yeah. But something tells me, with those two men, it'd be completely different. There's such a sexy power about them," Nancy gushed. "I'm sure you can feel it too."

With a wince Morning refused to answer. "What are you doing today?"

"Oh, famous brush-off," Nancy answered. "That means you are *very* interested."

"Whatever. I'm chopping up vegetables, creating a salad, because I need food. I've been working in the studio all morning."

"I'm not doing anything. How about you make salad for two, and I'll bring over some chocolate cake."

"How can I refuse such an offer?" Morning asked with a laugh. "Get your ass over here. I'll put on coffee too."

At that, she hit the Off button on her phone and doubled the portions of her salad. She had originally planned on a big meatless Caesar, but then she went rummaging in the fridge and found a cold cooked chicken breast. Easy enough to slice and add that to the top. She was sprinkling the parmesan on the salad when Nancy walked in.

"The place is empty, huh?"

"Yeah," Morning said. "I haven't seen anybody but Geir and Jager this morning."

"How are they?"

"They look fine. They look normal." Morning smiled. "I don't think they were busy having one-night stands with anyone," she said drily.

"You wouldn't know that though, would you?"

"I would hope not," she said with a shudder. She wondered exactly what kind of woman Geir was after. Did he have a particular taste? She wondered if she would ever have passion like Nancy described. The one thing Morning wasn't good at was girl talk. She could do the manicure stuff and the clothing stuff; she could gush about boys when she was growing up, but she hadn't been able to do the same with the subject of sex. To her it was private. Something she enjoyed but kept as an intimate relationship with her partners.

Nancy, on the other hand, liked most men, except she wanted them to stick around longer than for just sex. Yet she kept returning to the same bad choices.

"Did you hear from any of your job applications?" Morning asked, trying to keep the subject on neutral territory. Nancy was a little too interested in her guests. It was nice that she had directed her attention at Jager because, for some reason, Morning had already notched out Geir as her own. But he didn't belong to anybody, and he never would. Something was untamed about him. He might have been badly hurt in an accident, but he was very much a predator.

She rolled that term around on her tongue, wondering if it fit, and then nodded. It didn't matter whether she thought about a lion or a silverback gorilla or Geir, something was very territorial about him, them. She'd never seen him in action, but she imagined he wouldn't tolerate anybody crossing the line. Including his partner.

"No, I didn't hear anything yet," Nancy said, sitting down on a bar stool at the island. "It's frustrating. We do all these résumés in the hope somebody will stop and take a look. But how many actually do? The whole job-hunt system is so different now."

"Right. Didn't you have to do an online interview with your last job application?"

"I did. And that was weird. It was a video conference, and I couldn't get the video part to work from my end. Technology is perfect when it works, but it sucks when it doesn't." Nancy looked at the salad. "Do you have any bread to go with that?"

Morning chuckled. "Are you hungry today or something?"

"Or something," she said agreeably.

Morning obliged by bringing over the loaf of bread, at least the center portion left from the men's breakfast yesterday morning. She cut a couple slices and brought out the tub of butter. Nancy transferred the chicken to her bread and dug into the salad. "Why did I put your chicken on the salad if you were just going to take it off?"

Nancy shrugged. "Yeah, why did you? Makes no sense to me."

Wrangling gently, as friends do, and they certainly did for much of the last five years, they ate together with their discussion on everything from jobs to men to shoes and then back to the gallery offer.

"How many paintings will you have ready?"

Irritated at being asked the same question she'd been trying to avoid this whole time, Morning shrugged. "I don't know. I have two and a half right now, but one is weird." She tilted her head and thought about it. "I may have three. Two are similar, but then yesterday I got upset, and I painted out all my anger and frustration, and now I'm not exactly sure if it's good or if it's bad."

"After dessert I want to see them," Nancy announced.

Morning eyed her friend over her coffee cup with resigned amusement. "I'm not sure I'm ready to let you see them."

Nancy stopped chewing and looked at Morning in surprise. "Why not? I love your work."

"Well, that's the problem. You love the *old* work. This is very different. And I don't know that anybody'll love this."

"I definitely want to see them now." Nancy reached over, cut herself a piece of the chocolate cake she'd brought with her and picked it up with her hand. She ate it as she sat at the island. "Hurry up. I want a first viewing of your paintings."

Morning rolled her eyes; then she remembered what the men were up to. "What do you know about Mr. Henderson?"

"Changing the topic to that odd teacher who's been around since way too long won't get you out of showing me the paintings."

"Is he decent?" Morning asked, her voice low.

Nancy shrugged. "I think so. He's friendly, popular. But to me, he's strange. Not very happy."

"Why? Because he's so old?" Morning looked at her

friend in surprise.

Nancy shook her head. "I don't mind the age. And, of course, happiness is a right, no matter what the age. There's just something icky about the way he looks at people."

"Please explain," Morning said. "I don't know that I've ever met him." At least that wasn't a direct lie because she had only known *of* Poppy way back when.

"Just creepy. The kids love him though, and I presume that's why the school keeps him around."

"Was there ever any talk about getting rid of him?"

Nancy shook her head. "No, not likely, but I'm not really in the know," she said apologetically. "Remember? I'm just a temp there—and a new one. Hence another taking my place who was the normal fill in substitute. Yet also, because of that, people do often speak as if I'm part of the woodwork and aren't careful about what they're saying."

"What did you hear?" Morning leaned closer, eager for any titbits.

Only Nancy shrugged. "Nothing really. Just that he was too friendly with the kids. A couple of the teachers were concerned."

"Right. The trouble with that is, nobody does anything because it's not quite bad enough, and nobody wants to cause trouble for themselves or for the teacher," Morning said in frustration. "And then ten, twenty, even thirty years later, we find out these teachers had long strings of abuses, and nobody spoke up to defend the children."

Nancy laughed. "There's your imagination going crazy again. I don't think he's done anything like that."

Morning kept her thoughts to herself. She stood, cleaned away the dishes, refused to have a piece of cake at the moment but refilled both coffee cups. She turned to her friend. "Against my better judgment, let's go up and take a look at the canvases."

THE TWO MEN once again did a full recon in the neighborhood with Poppy's second house. They kept an eye out, checking the demographics. In this case, the home appeared to be half of a duplex. Not a house owned singularly by one person. Duplexes were not common in this area. It was also an odd choice for a pedophile because, if he had children in here, somebody could hear through the walls. On the other hand, both halves of the duplex appeared to be empty. "If we think it's important we could look into who the owner of the second half is," Jager said. "Both sides appear empty. And would be a better bet to enter through."

"Already on it." Geir's fingers moved rapidly on his phone's keypad. "It's coming up as Vitus Chan. He purchased it a year ago."

"So maybe it's an investment property or is planning to move in soon?"

They walked up to the front door on the neighbor's side and knocked. Nobody answered. They walked around to the back of the house but couldn't see any signs of recent habitation. No vehicles were parked in front or back, and, though a fence divided the respective yards to the two halves, both appeared to be empty. It was supposed to be a rancher, they thought. But it was surprising that it ended up being a duplex.

"This is a weird setup."

"It is."

Standing at the back door to the other side of the duplex, they couldn't see any of the neighbors because of the trees and a wooden privacy fence. Plus the door was designed as a wind protector that blocked their view even more.

Making a quick decision, Geir knocked on the back door and heard no answer. He tested the door, but it was locked. He pulled his tool kit from his back pocket and had the door open in seconds. He stepped inside, calling out, "Hello, anyone home?"

There was only silence. The two men walked through the small space; this side of the duplex appeared to be no more than one thousand square feet. Probably the same for Poppy's side of the duplex.

"This is kind of a waste. You'd think, for this neighborhood, it would be better developed."

"Depends who built it and when. It could have been a long time ago."

Geir nodded. "Hopefully we can get some details on that soon enough." As they walked through, he shrugged. "No furniture, no food. It's definitely an empty space."

It looked like it hadn't been used in a long time. Frowning, they stopped and studied the wall that separated them from the other half of the duplex.

"Too bad there isn't a connecting door."

"No, there may not be a connecting door, but I wonder if we can get up in the attic? I know the house itself has been divided into two residences, but it was likely a single dwelling at one time."

Geir looked at Jager in surprise, heading into the master bedroom, opening the closet. "Most of the time their attic access is through a closet."

"Sure, but this is California, and anything goes in a place like this. So many places have been dropped and rebuilt.

Others converted as was convenient."

"I guess that's what I mean about it's odd that this place is empty. I wonder why such a small house? It's prime real estate, and a larger house would have definitely made more sense in terms of resale value."

"It is what it is."

Geir pointed up to a small trapdoor at the far end of the master bedroom closet, a closet that wasn't even big enough in his mind for a house this size.

Jager was taller than Geir by a couple inches. Jager managed to pop the trapdoor and slide it off to the side. Geir held his hands cupped as he bent slightly. Jager put a foot in them, and Geir boosted Jager up so he could take a look into the attic space.

"Does it connect?" Geir asked.

"I'll be back in a minute. I'll let you know." Jager went through the trapdoor, his feet the last to disappear into the darkness above. There was no chair or anything for Geir to pull himself up on. He could jump and get in, but there was no point if Jager didn't find a way across to Poppy's half of the duplex.

Shortly thereafter Jager's face popped into the hole, and, with a big smile, he said, "There's a trapdoor on Poppy's side of the building."

Geir swung his arms up and jumped, pulling himself up with difficulty into the attic. He sat there straddling the opening for a moment and said, "Sure do miss my foot sometimes."

"You mean, your *human* foot." Jager smiled.

"I mean, *mine*," Geir said for clarification. "It's one thing to have prosthetics to get around, but it's another thing to have them when you're doing this kind of work."

Jager was already halfway across the attic, walking carefully on the timbers so he didn't fall through the ceiling. The space was small, and he was crouched down low, trying to get to the other side.

Fiberglass was in between the framework, so falling through the ceiling or into the insulation would just end up hurting Geir or getting him itchy. He shrugged. Choosing to travel on his hands and knees, he joined Jager on the far side. And, indeed, there was a trapdoor, exactly the same as they'd come through.

Jager soundlessly lifted it up, placing it on top of the struts. He leaned forward and peered in. Coming back up again, he said, "It goes into the master bedroom, same as the other side. Stay here. I'll be back in five."

Jager lowered himself into the closet, landing so softly that Geir had a hard time hearing Jager's movements. Geir edged over to the hole. He waited for a few minutes, studying the closet and the clothes here: hanging suits, shoes, all male apparel stacked in the closet. Nothing that he could see as being female. The shelves held a few items and boxes. One of them looked to be a banker's box. The lid was off, and Geir could see envelopes inside. He was desperate to take a closer look.

Jager suddenly appeared below. "The place is empty."

After Jager stepped out, Geir nodded and slid into the closet. As he stood here, he grabbed the banker's box, put it on the floor and turned on the light in the closet, taking a closer look. "Holy shit," he whispered under his breath.

But Jager was already gone.

Geir did a full sweep of the closet to see if anything else here should be double-checked. Then he focused again on the box. In it was paperwork, but, more than that, there were photographs. Mouse had definitely been here and had spent a lot of time here, as proven by a lot of Mouse's childhood memories, growing-up memories, stored away in this box. Had Poppy kept them for Mouse? Or were they mementoes that Poppy had wanted to keep when Mouse was intent on throwing them out?

Geir shook his head. "Aah, Mouse, you spent time here. Lots of it. Or stored your memories here at least. Or rather Poppy did." Mouse had never mentioned having a place like this to go to. If anything, while on leave, he was always talking about going to some third-world country for vacations.

Had he ever gone to Libya, Somalia, Sudan? Or had he just come back to California? Nobody would have been the wiser. How long had Mouse expected to maintain that lie? But then to have even gotten as far as he had in life with such a background, obviously he was one hell of a liar. It completely amazed Geir just how different the Mouse they knew was from the person they were finding here. And Geir wondered about a man who lived with such hollow beginnings and such emptiness inside that he needed to create another persona in order to survive. Or was this deception something Mouse enjoyed?

Geir looked around for other paperwork but didn't find any. He squatted beside the box, carefully lifted out envelope after envelope. He emptied one to see pictures, and he winced. They were all images of men in sexual positions. And, in every one of them, Mouse stared back at him.

"Oh, Mouse, I'm so sorry you didn't feel like you could tell us."

They'd all known he was gay. They'd all protected and closed ranks around him because he was one of them. But to have had such a childhood and to have not been able to share that with them? Maybe he would have given more time, or maybe he wouldn't have trusted them to that extent.

Geir realized then that most of the men in the photos were the same one or two men. And one of them was older. Geir stared at the photo and thought it could be the teacher from the current online photo.

He flipped over the photograph and found the name *Poppy* and the year written on the back. Geir studied it for a long time, realizing this had to be the same man who had groomed Mouse since he was young. Mouse appeared to be at least twenty-five in this set of photographs, though Geir could be off by a couple years. Although Minx had stated that Mouse would be thirty now. They didn't even know for sure if Mouse was the age he had claimed to be while in the navy. His driver's license found at Poppy's first house, issued five years ago, gave his DOB, but was it his actual date of birth or a fake ID?

As he squatted here, Geir sent Levi a question, asking to confirm Mouse's DOB and if there was a record of Mouse changing his name while in the military. It might be a question better put to Mason instead.

Geir pulled up another envelope from the very bottom and found a birth certificate. It was, believe it or not, for Mickey Mouse. Mickey Mouse O'Connor. Geir stared at it. So Minx out of Texas had been right. Mouse would have been thirty this year, and his legal name was Mickey Mouse. God, what kind of parent would do that to a child? Geir took a photograph of the name and then the document itself.

Next he found a picture of Minx. He took a photograph of that, realizing, at one point, Mouse had thought of his childhood friend. Geir came across other documents he didn't recognize, but he photographed everything he found and returned it all to the box, then reshelved it. With another glance around, he saw nothing of value.

Until he found a photograph in an envelope under some T-shirts on another shelf.

Jager came back at that time. "I didn't see anything else of interest."

Geir nodded. "I found lots, and it's all in that box. Mouse was legally Mickey Mouse O'Connor, just like Minx said. So this Mouse is her Mouse." He held up the photograph of a young man. "But take a close look. Who does he remind you of?"

Jager took one look and whistled. "That's our Mouse."

CHAPTER 10

MORNING LED THE way to her studio. Nancy had been here many times in the past. They chatted as they walked up.

"It feels empty in here today," Nancy said. "You've got such a big house. I often wondered how you felt when you were alone but then realized that most the time you weren't alone. Yet today ..."

Morning nodded. "It does feel empty today. Maybe that's a good thing. I've had some difficult self-reflection moments, making me a little less confident in what I'm doing."

Nancy looked at her friend in surprise. "What do you mean?"

Morning hesitated. "It's kind of hard to explain, but the house has always been my hideaway. It's my safety net. But more than that, it's been a haven for me. I hadn't recognized how much I put stock in that concept until my father discussed maybe selling. And, of course, my father wants his money from it, and, since I'm not making enough money to pay him for his half, I will likely have to sell. And every time I think about selling, it makes my stomach cramp, as pure panic hits."

"I can understand that."

Morning shrugged. "I can understand it theoretically

too. But emotionally … it's like a visceral attack on my gut." She took out her keys and unlocked the studio door, pushed it open and turned on the lights.

Nancy walked to the pretty pictures and smiled. "I've always loved these."

"Of course you have, but those aren't the new paintings," Morning said drily. She walked Nancy around to the easel. "This is my current one, the half-done one that I'm finishing up."

Nancy's jaw dropped. She stepped back farther, shook her head and leaned closer. "Wow."

Morning stood off to the side. She held her coffee with one hand, but she shoved the other into her pocket, rocking on her heels. "What does *wow* mean?" she asked nervously.

Nancy slid a glance her way, then zinged her focus back to the painting. "You don't know?"

Morning shrugged. "I'm very insecure about my painting, as you know."

"Well, you sure as hell don't need to be. This is freakin' unbelievable."

Nancy stepped forward as if it would give her added clarity. She shook her head and stepped back. "I don't understand that glow. But it's like a translucent light. And, because of the fog, it's like something's trying to break free. If I could just get closer, I could see it, but I can't see it because of the fog."

Morning smiled. "I know. I'm not sure what to call it yet, or the entire series, but there is something very different about it." She motioned to Nancy. "Now close your eyes, and I'll switch out the painting."

Morning lifted the cityscape, resting it on the floor, and brought up the first one with the blossoms, putting it on the easel. "Okay, you can open your eyes."

Nancy's eyes flew open, and her jaw dropped. "I don't even know what to say. Oh, my God, that's absolutely stunning."

Pleased and feeling relief wash through her as she admitted that maybe she wasn't prejudiced about her own artwork, she stepped beside Nancy and looked at the light coming through on the painting. "This is the first one I did. And I wasn't exactly sure what the hell I'd done, so I was trying to repeat it or to do something similar, when I did the first one you saw."

Nancy reached out, her fingers opening and closing. "I really, really, *really* want that one. But I think you could sell that for thousands of dollars."

Morning's eyebrows shot up. "Do you think so?" She was cautious with her words. "A part of me wants to believe that, but, at the same time, I'm concerned I'm fooling myself."

"Well, you certainly got me fooled then," Nancy said. "I've never seen work like this before. The use of light, it's... unique." She frowned. "I swear to God I didn't even know you had this in you." She turned to look at her friend. "You should be very proud."

Morning felt a warmth wash through her heart as she took in her friend's compliments, listened for that voice of truth and realized she really was hearing it. She gave a happy sigh. "Thank you. I was so afraid they were no good."

"*No good*? Oh, my God! They're fantastic." Nancy looked greedily around the room. "Are there any more?"

"Well, there is the third one, the weird one," Morning said. "Close your eyes again." Nancy closed her eyes, but, at the same time, she snapped her heels together and froze.

Morning laughed. "It's not that bad." She brought up the red painting. As she placed it on the easel, she said, "Now remember. This one isn't meant to be anything. It's just an abstract."

"Can I open my eyes?" Nancy asked impatiently.

"Okay, open them."

Nancy opened them, and her eyes grew wider and wider. She stared at the painting for a long moment. "How can you say it doesn't represent anything?"

Morning, not sure of her reaction, studied her friend's face. "What are you talking about?"

Nancy stepped closer and reached out. "I thought at first it was a self-portrait or something—but in an abstract way—because look at the two women." She leaned into the canvas, tilting her head. "No, it's a man and a woman."

Frowning, not having a clue what Nancy was talking about, Morning stepped up beside her friend and studied the painting. And she saw it for herself, almost in a yin-yang symbol from the circles. Caught up through the layers of the red strokes was an abstract male and female face. She stood and stared at it for a long moment.

Nancy looked at her. "Didn't you plan on that?"

Morning shook her head. "Not really. What I was trying to do was express the emotions I was feeling at the time."

"What kind of emotions?" Nancy shook her head. "There's a lot of red, a lot of cream and that light again. The use of light on these three paintings is stunning. Yes, this one's incredibly different from the other two, but I like it just as well." She stared at it. "Honestly, maybe I like it a little more, but it's so hard to say because they're all freaking fantastic."

Overwhelmed by her friend's enthusiasm, Morning

smiled. "Well, then I won't feel quite so bad about taking them to the gallery owner tomorrow."

"You better not feel bad at all," Nancy said. "I'd love to come with you so I could see his face."

"And maybe you can at that. I don't know. You're the only one who has seen these three. Well, Geir saw the first one too."

Nancy pounced. "Geir has?"

Morning nodded. "Yes. Not that I invited him in, but he was looking for me and somehow managed to come in when I was working on the cherry blossom one."

Nancy motioned at the *pretty* pictures. "I've always loved those. They could hang in my kitchen and living room or anywhere. But these three new ones are intense. I just can't stop staring at them. I can't tell which one I like the most because they are so different. That fog one is really special because it keeps sucking me in, but this one with that hidden meaning through the color …" She shook her head. "Wow."

Morning chuckled. "You've just made my day. Thank you." She walked to the double French doors that were still open. "I guess I can close these now. The smell in here is not too bad, is it?"

Nancy shook her head. "I didn't notice when I came in. It's a good space for you because you can open those doors."

"I should have either a ventilation system or a much bigger room. But I don't have the space, not if I need the rooms for guests."

"The rooms are income. But I tell you, sweetie, you get a handhold in the art market with these, and you won't have to have a bed-and-breakfast anymore."

"Oh, I don't think it'll be that easy." Morning smiled. "The thing is, these are something I'm not even sure I can repeat every time I pick up a paintbrush. Right now I'm worried the next thing I do won't have the same luminescence behind it."

"The only way to do that is to keep painting," Nancy said. "I believe in you. I always have because I love those first paintings of yours. But these, Jesus, they are an entire level above."

Morning smiled to herself. She stood looking at her backyard for a long moment and then, hearing a sound, turned around. She glanced at Nancy and asked, "Did you hear that?"

Nancy shook her head, her gaze still on the red painting in front of her. "Honestly I'm not listening to anything. I swear to God this painting is talking to me."

Morning laughed. "I thought I heard something downstairs."

"It's possible. You've got lots of people staying here."

"But I didn't hear the bells to announce anybody had come home yet." Morning motioned to the door. "Let's go refill our coffees."

Nancy shook her head. "Hell no." She held out her cup. "You go refill both coffees. I'll stand here and admire your artwork."

Laughing, yet eminently pleased at her friend's response, Morning agreed. She grabbed the two empty cups and headed down the back stairs to the kitchen.

As she walked past her father's room, she thought she heard another sound. Frowning, she placed the coffee cups on the kitchen table and went back. Using her key, she popped open the door and turned on the light. And froze. The bedding had been tossed on the floor, and the place appeared to be in shambles.

"What happened?" she cried in shock.

Then somebody barreled toward her, slamming her up against the hallway wall as he raced past her. Her head snapped against the wall behind her, and she cried out. The intruder tore down the hall and burst through the front door.

Sitting on the floor for a long moment, her mind tried to put together what had happened. Shaky, she pulled out her phone and texted Geir. She didn't even question why she was contacting him and not somebody else, but she knew he was the one to call. She realized her fingers weren't texting properly and just hit Dial. Within seconds his phone rang. When she heard his voice, she burst into tears.

"Morning, what's the matter?"

She took several bracingly deep gulping breaths before she could form words. "There was an intruder in the house," she said quietly, striving for a calmness she didn't feel. "He slammed into me before he raced out the front door."

"When? Just now?"

"Yes," she said. "Nancy is upstairs in my studio. I came down to get more coffee and heard a noise in my father's rooms. I unlocked the door, and he came flying at me."

"Any idea why he was in your father's rooms?"

"I'd say he's looking for something, but I don't know what. The bedding has been tossed and so has some of the furniture."

"We're on our way home," Geir said quietly. "Grab your coffee, go back upstairs and lock yourself into your studio with Nancy, okay? Don't ask questions. Just do it. We'll be right there."

She took another shaky breath, managing to get to her feet. She pocketed her phone, went into the kitchen, refilled the coffee cups. Mindful of his orders and never doubting the sense behind them, she hurried back upstairs to the studio. She stepped inside, put the cups down, turned and shut the door casually, locking it in the process. She gave Nancy a big smile. "Well, that was interesting."

Nancy was still staring at the painting. She tore her gaze away from the canvas. "What's the matter?"

Morning looked at her and sighed. "I just had a brush with an intruder."

Nancy stared at her for a long moment and then said, "Really?"

Morning's bottom lip trembled as she nodded. Nancy swept over, wrapped her in a hug and said, "Oh, my God! I'm so glad you're okay."

Morning wrapped her arms around her friend and burst into tears.

GEIR DROVE FAST. "It doesn't make any sense. Why the hell would he be back in her father's room?"

"He's looking for the mouse," Jager said. "I don't know who this asshole is or why he's tormenting her and us, but I swear to God he's after the stuffed mouse."

"It makes sense, but it's not like there's anything inside the mouse." Then he turned a corner, approaching a set of traffic lights. He slowed and waited. "Or I missed something when she showed it to me," Geir said. "I took a good look but didn't feel anything inside, and there was no obvious stitching showing. She returned it to the hall closet, but it doesn't make sense that it had something inside it."

"I know. None of this makes sense," Jager added. "We

knew him as Ryan Hanson, but he only wanted to be called Mouse. So, when Mouse stepped into Ryan's life, I guess he kept Mouse as a nickname. And, if we accept all this, then we have to accept that this Mouse we've been tracking is the man we trained with and worked with for a year. This same Mouse had a very strange relationship with a pedophile who likely helped Mouse forge documents to get into the navy and into the SEALs program by taking someone's place after that person passed BUD/S training."

"But," Geir continued, "the pedophile had to have had connections to find out who had successfully completed BUD/S training, of which there's very rarely more than one or two, and he'd have to know what that person's plans were in order to take him out and put Mouse in his place."

"It would take the right chain of events for it all to work," Jager admitted. "The chances of getting caught? *Huge.*"

"And why would Poppy help Mouse?" Geir asked. "Because he'd lose Mouse then."

"Unless he truly loved Mouse, and it was a big dream of Mouse's, and Poppy was determined to help Mouse. And maybe, when Mouse went on leave, he went home to Poppy."

"That's a very sad, twisted relationship," Geir said.

"Sure, but, at this point, Mouse was happy with it or so conditioned that he didn't see anything wrong with it, … or he was using it to get what he wanted himself," Jager said very slowly.

"It's all messed up," Geir muttered. He managed to get through the next traffic light, but the traffic got heavier. He took a quick detour, whipped around several blocks and cut a corner at another big intersection. Back on the road, and only a few blocks away from Morning's house, he said, "I still don't understand why whoever is doing this would have put a toy mouse into her father's room."

"That's what we have to figure out. That and what relationship that person had with our Mouse and with Poppy. But I have to assume someone knows we're here and is doing it for our sake and not hers. But how? And why?"

"The *why* will have something to do with our investigation. The *how*? I'm not sure." Geir frowned, then shook his head. "Except Mason paid for the rooms with *his* credit card. ... Not ours."

Jager didn't say anything.

But, in the back of Geir's mind, he knew it would be easy enough to track credit cards. That this asshole might have considered Mason was involved in this case—now that was interesting. But then, along with Levi, both had been instrumental in getting them this far with their investigation. But how would anyone know—unless he was the one they were tracking. ... So was Poppy their killer, discounting that the winos said otherwise? Poppy certainly loved Mouse. And had the naval connections ...

"Poppy has a lot to answer for," Geir said, "but he's not likely to be the guy breaking into Morning's place. She said she saw somebody running across her backyard yesterday, but didn't think it was important enough to tell us about."

"Why would she? Think about it. She doesn't know us from anybody else."

"But she does know Mason, and that is huge. Mason vouched for us. She's willing to trust him." Geir pulled up in front of the bed-and-breakfast. They hopped out and jogged to the front door, which was wide open. As they stepped through, a man in a suit stood there, looking around. Geir immediately felt the hairs on the back of his neck go up. "Can I help you?"

The businessman turned to look at him. "I'm looking for Morning. I'm checking out today and need her to finish the registration form."

Geir nodded. This had to be the single guest. "I just spoke to her on the phone. She's probably in her studio. I'll be right back." Leaving Jager here to deal with the guest, Geir walked through to the kitchen and up the back stairs. At the studio he knocked on the door. "Morning, it's me."

The door unlocked while he waited, and, when it opened, he took one look at her tear-stained face and sighed. He opened his arms, and she ran into them. He held her tight. "I'm so sorry. I wish that hadn't happened."

She nodded but didn't say a word. Her arms were wrapped tight around him. He hugged her until she was calm enough to release him.

Then he brushed her hair off her face and smiled. "I think one of your guests is downstairs wanting to leave."

She tried to get a more business-like look on her face and nodded. "I'll deal with it." She wiped her eyes and walked into her bedroom.

Nancy came to stand beside him, her gaze curious. "Is it safe to leave yet?"

He nodded. "We're back now."

She smiled and said, "Take good care of her." And she ran down the stairs.

He waited until Morning came back out. Her hair was fixed up, and her face was freshly washed, so it didn't look like she'd been ravaged by tears. It wasn't a bad freshen-up job for having been so rushed. Maybe nobody would notice she'd been crying.

Downstairs, she walked through the hall. He kept her in his sights the whole time.

She smiled at the guest. "Time to leave, Ken?"

He nodded. "I thought I was staying tonight. I'm sorry, but I need to leave now." He looked at his watch. "I've got to be at the airport in an hour."

"No problem." She filled out the paperwork, ran his credit card and handed him a receipt.

Geir and Jager sat down in the living room, where they could keep an eye on what was going on. As soon as Ken was done, he smiled, gave a nod to the two men, turned and walked out.

There was something about him. He was a little too nice. He smiled a little too friendly, or maybe it was Morning's smile that was a little too friendly in response. Jager's voice beside Geir pulled him out of his reverie.

"Down, boy."

Geir stared at him. "What are you talking about?"

Jager just chuckled.

Geir hopped to his feet and asked Morning, "Who do you still have here?"

"I haven't seen the couple all day." She frowned. "I don't know what they're up to. I don't even know for sure they came home last night," she confessed. She stared at the staircase for a long moment, snatched up her keys and said, "I'll knock and see if they're here."

"You do take people's credit card information, so they can't bolt and not pay you, right?"

"I precharge for one full night, and then they're supposed to pay the balance before they leave," she said as she walked up the stairs.

Jager wandered through the downstairs, but Geir

wouldn't let her out of his sight. "Where was Ken staying?"

She pointed to the back room on the second floor. "He was in there."

"And where is the couple staying?"

She went down the hall. "They're in this room." She walked up to the door and knocked on it. No answer. She called out, "Hello, are you in there?" Still no answer. She grabbed her key and, without hesitation, unlocked the door. She pulled it open and looked inside. The bedcovers were a mess, but there was no sign of anyone. She frowned. "I don't know what to think."

"What do you mean? Do you think they've left?" Geir stepped into the room and looked around. "There's no luggage."

"Check the closet. Lots of people put their clothing away."

He walked to the closet, and, sure enough, it was empty. He turned to look at her. "What's the chance they've bolted on you?"

She crossed her arms over her chest. "It's never happened before."

"You didn't see them today at all?"

She shook her head. "No, they were supposed to be here for two nights."

"And they might have been because they certainly could have left today. If there's nobody downstairs to keep track, it's basically an honor system, isn't it?"

She frowned at him. "Don't you start with me too," she scolded. "I've already had a tough enough day." Depressed, she stared around the room.

He watched her.

She stepped back out of the room. "Well, I'll wait until

tomorrow. If they don't show up, then I'll charge the room to their credit card."

"What are the rules that you have them sign?"

"They're supposed to check out at eleven in the morning, but there was no sign of them this morning." She frowned more. "But then they didn't come for breakfast either morning."

Geir nodded. He wondered if this was just a simple case of trying to skip out on a second night or if they were off somewhere else. The other option was, they were here for nefarious reasons and didn't want to be seen. There was an awful lot one could get away with in a bed-and-breakfast. Somebody would have to call around to each and every bed-and-breakfast in a particular area to find out where the couple were booked. "And you said you know these two?"

She stared at him for a long moment. "They said they were here a couple years ago, that they loved it so much they came back." She sighed. "But honestly I didn't remember them. I did spend some time visiting with them the first day they were here, but that was just being social."

"They could have said anything they wanted to. But what difference would it make whether you knew them or not?"

"Return visitors always get priority. And, because I am alone here, I do take some precautions. I don't like to make reservations for people I don't know or who don't have references."

"But you didn't know Ken, did you?"

She shook her head. "No. Business hasn't been all that great because I don't do a ton of advertising. Generally people find me through word of mouth, and I've been taking them in because I've needed the money. So, for all I know, the couple said that so they could get in. I don't know."

Geir stared at her and then gave a clipped nod. "I hear you, but you need to change your system."

She nodded sadly. "I feel like an era has just passed."

CHAPTER 11

MORNING CERTAINLY HADN'T been lying when she had said it felt as if an era had passed, and it wasn't fair. She was dealing with a loss of innocence right now. A mind-set that she felt she would never regain. It also left her chilled inside. She glanced at Geir. "I guess I just learned my lesson." She watched his gaze narrow.

He shrugged. "I'm sure being in business and stiffed for a bill is not an uncommon prospect. I'm more concerned about your safety."

"I can understand that," she said quietly. "I'm more than a little disturbed that people have come into my house other than to stay. It's hard to know who would do this or why."

"It's possibly because of us," he admitted. "It's too early to tell. But we came here hunting a man, the one you know as Poppy. And a friend of ours was seen leaving Texas with him. His name was Mouse."

She stared at him in surprise. "That's why you're here?"

He nodded. "Mason knows us and vouched for us because we were in the same naval unit with him. When we needed a place to stay that was close enough and that would allow us anonymity, he suggested your place."

She nodded. "I've had others, his friends, come here and stay too, plus men who worked for Levi." She frowned. "Or maybe it was for Legendary Security."

Geir grinned. "Yes, Levi is a good friend of ours too."

"Nice that you have friends in high places."

"They've been very helpful and have assisted us in tracking down these men."

"And why would you track them down? What have they done?"

He shoved his hands in his pockets, leaned against a doorjamb and stared at her.

She stared back calmly. "You might not want to tell me, but, if there's any chance this involves me or my place, then I need to know."

He glanced around the room. "I don't think it has anything to do with this couple or anyone else staying here ..." His voice trailed off, then he added, "But ..."

"There was only Ken and the couple here," she said. "And Ken is gone now."

His gaze zipped back toward her. "Ken. Do you know anything about him?"

"I don't get people to fill out an occupation survey when I let them in," she said in exasperation. "People come to San Diego for a lot of reasons. It's not up to me to sort out why."

"Did he ever move around the house, go into any of the spaces he wasn't welcome in?"

She frowned. "No more than you did," she snapped. "He came up to the studio once, but that was it."

"Your studio, right." He grinned. "Do I get to see the other paintings?"

Now it was her turn to shove her hands in her pockets. She shrugged. "Maybe. I do need to get up there and finish working."

"How many have you done?"

Irritated and not sure how to get the conversation back

on track, she said, "Three. And I'll tell you what. I'll show you my paintings, but I want the full story out of you."

"Then how about we take a cup of coffee to your studio, and I'll explain it. I definitely want to make sure our conversation is private, so nobody can overhear us."

She went into the kitchen, put on yet another pot and, when it was done dripping, poured two large mugs. "Let's go."

It took them a few seconds to reach her studio. On the way he said, "What do you want to do about the room?"

She tossed him a look. "What do you want me to do? It's not like I can call the police and say the visitors absconded without payment."

"Can't you?"

She frowned, then shrugged. "Maybe. I don't know."

"I meant, what do you want to do about your father's rooms?"

She winced. "I'll have to straighten everything. But after my gallery meeting."

"Where's the stuffed mouse?"

"It's still in the hall closet. I haven't touched it," she said. She gave him her coffee cup to hold as she pulled out her keys and unlocked the studio.

He nodded and waited.

Finally she had the door open and pushed it wide, turned on the light and said, "I need a filtration system of some kind." She walked across the room and opened up the double French doors. When she turned back, he still stood in the doorway, his gaze searching the room. "What are you looking for?"

"Any sign your intruder came in here."

She stared at him in shock. "I found my studio unlocked, but why would he have come in here?"

"Would anybody willfully try to hurt you?"

She shook her head. "No, of course not. I don't have any enemies." Yet she could feel her stomach knotting and her heart sinking. "But, if I did, and they destroyed my paintings … I'd be in deep trouble because the gallery owner will be pissed at me, never take me at my word again," she said, walking over, taking a cup of coffee from him. "Plus, I'd be devastated if something happened to these paintings."

"So do I get to see them?"

She said, "Come over here, and stand in front of the easel. I'll put them on one at a time."

He nodded, standing in front of the empty easel, sipping his coffee.

"Close your eyes."

He did.

Making sure he wasn't cheating, she put up the first one. "This is the one you saw but wasn't quite finished."

He opened his eyes, studied it and smiled. "It's still as spectacular as when I first saw it. You're very talented."

She snorted. "Hardly. What I am is pleased." Pleased he appeared to be sincere. "Then I tried to repeat that same odd light effect. Close your eyes and I'll show you the second one."

She removed the blossom picture and replaced it with the foggy cityscape. When it was in place, she said, "Okay, now take a look." Instead of looking at the picture, she watched his face. As he opened his eyes and comprehended what was in front of him, his face lit up. "Wow, that's fantastic."

He took a couple steps closer, so he could look at it more in depth. "It's breathtaking."

"Thank you. I'm happy to hear that. It's very unusual for me," she said a little nervously. "And I'm unsure of exactly what I'm doing."

"Sure, it's something new. It's something different, but that certainly doesn't make it wrong. Did you say you had three of them?"

"Well, the other one is even odder. It's an abstract. I don't generally do abstract," she said with a half laugh.

"I'd like to see it."

She nodded and removed the cityscape and put it back on the floor, turned to look at him and said, "Close your eyes."

He chuckled but again closed his eyes obligingly.

She picked up the big red abstract and put it in place, then stepped back, taking another look herself. Would he see the faces or would he see something completely different? "Okay, open your eyes."

She watched as he opened his eyes and stared at the painting. Instead of a cry, a *Wow*, or *How wonderful*, he was silent. Nervous, she clutched at her coffee cup, looking at him instead of the painting.

He leaned closer. "I've never seen anything like it."

"Maybe that's good? It's still got the weird lighting thing going on, but I did it more as an outlet for the stress and emotion I was dealing with at the time."

"Sounds like being stressed is a good thing for you then."

She realized he thought it was decent. "Do you think it's okay?" She hated that she needed reassurance but was aware she was still so far away from being confident that she did need it.

"It's more than okay," he said quietly. "It's got a depth

to it that, the longer I stare at it, the more I see. But the faces in there"—he continued to stare at it—"they kind of sneak into the back of your head and stay there."

At that, she chuckled. "I didn't even see it at first. Nancy pointed out the faces to me."

He turned to look at her and said in amazement, "Are you telling me that you didn't plan that?"

She shook her head. "No, I so didn't."

"Wow. Okay. Well, you need to keep painting. That's where your talent lies, and there's so much more to you than what you've had a chance to explore."

"I think that's true with any artist. Once you explore new avenues, you learn more, can do more. I've dabbled in painting, but I stuck to nice. I stuck to pretty. I didn't allow anything with depth to come out."

"Any idea why it's coming out this time?"

"Frustration, fear, insecurity, questioning my life, my future." She laughed at her words, then turned to watch him walking around the easel to study her other paintings. "Mostly I think it was tension. Uncertainty."

"Well, whatever was bothering you led you to create a masterpiece, converting that angst into something very special."

"I think a lot of people paint to get rid of their emotions. It's hard to say if this is something I can do on an ongoing basis though. If the gallery owner wants more than one showing like this, I'm not sure I have it in me."

"You have it in you. But what you have to do is let go of the outcome of what it is you'll produce."

That startled a laugh out of her. "That's very insightful."

He gave her a lopsided grin. "No, not really. I used to play the guitar when I was young, before I went into the

GEIR

navy. I often thought I should be a musician and write songs. But I haven't gone back to that in a long time. At the time though, I used to sit back, close my eyes and just let my fingers play whatever they wanted to play. And what came out was often completely different from what I would have expected. And sometimes way nicer."

"I think that's true for every art form. It's a matter of trusting and letting go." She motioned to the door. "Shall we?"

He nodded. "What do you want to do about the room with the couple?"

"I should check my cell phone and the answering machine for the business landline to see if they left a message. Maybe this isn't something negative. Maybe they got called away suddenly."

"But the room is in rough shape."

"I know." She sighed. "But was that them, or was that like you said, the intruder from my father's room?" Locking the door behind her, she turned toward him. "Did you check your room, make sure it's okay?"

He shook his head. "But we can do that now." He led the way downstairs to his room, unlocked the door and stepped inside. As they walked in, he stopped. "Wow. Son of a bitch." His bedding had been dumped upside down too.

She gasped. "Has somebody gone through all the rooms? What were they looking for?"

"I hate to say it, but I suspect it's the mouse."

He walked to Jager's adjoining room, opened the door and stepped in, flicking on the lights. "Same thing."

She raced in behind him. "Oh, my God! Oh, my God!"

"Good thing we don't keep anything here that's important."

"Do you think he was after anything else?"

"Doesn't matter if he was or not. We don't keep IDs or laptops or anything like that behind. Those are always with us."

She bit her bottom lip, sighed. "You know I hate to ask because I enjoyed your visit, but, if your arrival brought this on, will your leaving take it away? And, if so, when are you leaving?" Her words were abrupt as she stared at the mess.

"It's possible the two are related. But it's not guaranteed."

She shook her head. "And how much of this has got something to do with Poppy?"

"Unfortunately too much. That's who we need to find."

She turned and walked out of the two rooms. She wasn't sure if she should say anything to him or not. But obviously he knew something was bothering her.

He gently gripped her shoulders. "It'll be okay."

She nodded. "I know it will, but I should let you know Poppy had a hideaway. At least that's what we called it."

"Where and what was it?"

She handed him a note with the name and address of the school on it. She shook her head. "I never attended school there, but at Rutler Elementary School, behind it, there's an equipment room where they stored all the soccer balls, mats and stuff for gym classes. Poppy used to spend a lot of time in there." She stared up at him. "That school isn't exactly the best in the city. In fact, it was probably the worst. It's an alternative school, so kids who don't fit into the regular system have a place to go."

"And what was Poppy's connection to it?"

"He used to run programs on Saturdays and sometimes after-school activities for the kids. Sports programs to get them outside, to give them an outlet for all their anger," she said in a mocking voice. "It was run by the community, and Poppy volunteered at this school and others around his teaching schedule."

"And you suspect that much more was going on?"

"Honestly I was blind to it back then because of my age. I certainly didn't say anything to anybody because one of the things you learn in that lifestyle is how people who tell get in trouble. But lots of kids knew."

GEIR STARED AT her for a moment.

"Was that helpful?"

He grinned, reached across and gave her a quick kiss on the lips. "Absolutely." Excitement surged through him as he headed down the second-floor hallway to the nearest set of stairs with a wave to Morning. "That's exactly what we were looking for, a hideaway. Someplace Poppy went to, preferably that not too many people knew about or used." He pulled out his phone and called Jager. "Where are you? We need to check out a new place."

"I'm walking up to the front door. Want to come down, and we'll head off?"

Geir was already running. He burst out the front door, saw Jager at the curb, waved and raced to the Jeep, that Jager already had running. Once inside, Geir said, "Morning said there was special place Poppy always went. A sports storage area behind the school."

"Midlands High School? Where he teaches at?"

Geir shook his head. "No, Rutler Elementary is an older one that's been shut down." He pulled a piece of paper from his pocket where she'd written down the address for him. "This is it." He punched it into the GPS. They watched as it came up on the screen.

"It's only ten minutes away." Jager turned the wheel and pulled the vehicle onto the street, heading off in the direction the GPS directed. "Are you thinking maybe he's still using this hiding place?"

"If he isn't using it still, maybe it has information from when he did use it," Geir said. "As we well know, men have habits and patterns, and they don't like to give up favorite places."

"Particularly if they are full of good memories," Jager said. "What I don't understand is how he's gotten away with it for so long."

"And why nobody has turned him in."

"Exactly. Sure, these kids are high-risk, but somebody should have been offended by it all."

"Unless he recognized kids who were confused about their own sexuality, choosing those kids over others."

"That tells us how young they were. In Mouse's case, didn't Minx say he was like twelve or fourteen?"

"But is that when it started?" Geir asked.

"No way to know," Jager said.

"Poppy didn't show up at school again today," Geir said.

"But the school is not worried, I bet. Chances are he does this off and on. He uses every last sick day he has available and any other holidays he can. Now, with us on his tail, he'll be extra careful."

"I don't doubt it. Chances are very good this guy has come to this point many times. He didn't survive all these decades without being very good at what he does."

They pulled into the school parking lot, seeing the ruts

and weeds coming through the pavement. The school was a very small building. "So, if it's no longer a school, what happened?"

"It was shut down." Geir looked at the information on his phone. "It was deemed too small, with expenses too large to fix it when they needed a new larger one. But, typical of a school board, they haven't sold off the property yet."

A gate blocked them from getting onto the grounds outside of the parking lot. They hopped out and walked the fence all the way around. "There has to be a way in."

And there was. They found a back gate. And it wasn't locked. They opened it, entered and closed it behind them, walking a well-traveled path between two small fields. As an elementary school, it had a fenced-in playground and a very small playing field. But the grass was overgrown pretty much everywhere. Although there was an exterior path around both fields, it didn't appear to be recently traveled.

Geir looked around. "Looks like more traffic from this direction."

"Makes sense, so the kids don't have to walk around to the front."

They approached the broken-down building quietly, walked around it first, inspecting the double front doors with wire-screen-reinforced double-paned glass windows inset into the top half of each door. The fact these windows had not been broken into surprised them because there were no bars on the windows here. Yet the school building itself had bars on all the doors and its windows.

"That says a lot about the students, doesn't it?"

"More about the state of the neighborhood probably."

They kept walking until they came to a small door in the back. It was a steel exterior door. that looked like a maintenance door.

Jager tried the handle, but, of course, it was locked.

Geir pulled out his tool kit he kept in his back pocket. It took him a little longer than he expected, but he finally had the lock popped. They both stepped to the side, and Jager pulled open the door, with Geir jumping in low, his gaze sweeping the area. "All clear," he called out.

Jager stepped up behind him, and they closed the door. Instantly darkness fell. "Do you think they still have power?"

"I doubt it, but who knows?" Geir hit the switch, and, sure enough, light filled the room.

"I guess they have to for safety reasons for the parking lot area, if nothing else," Jager said.

They stared at a small storeroom, maybe ten foot by twelve, shelves on the side that contained a couple of flattened balls and pieces of garbage left behind. Two black mats were on the floor, but they were torn and ragged from use and the years. A bigger stack of them was against one of the walls.

Geir and Jager walked the small area, studying the contents. "Not a whole lot here," Geir said, disappointment in his voice. He wasn't sure what he'd expected, but he sure as hell had hoped they'd find something.

"I wish we had luminol spray," Jager said. "We should see all kinds of bodily fluids."

"A part of me is glad we don't," Geir said, spinning to look at Jager.

Jager stared at the mats stacked against a wall. He pulled one off the stack so the next one was showing, and, sure enough, it appeared to be covered in something.

Geir didn't even want to think about what. Particularly if he was thinking of a pedophile having used this space for his criminal activities.

"Maybe it's a good thing we don't have luminol," Jager said. He shook his head. "Never thought to bring anything like that."

"I know. If we had a reason to bring in the cops, that's a different story. They could do a full search. But we have to find some strong evidence in order for them to even bother coming to this location."

"In that case, let's turn this place upside down and see what's here."

And that's what they did. They took a good hour, moving shelves, looking at and underneath everything, inspecting the walls for writing, and, just as they were about to give up, they found it in the far corner.

Geir sat on the mats, having pulled them en masse out to the center of the room, and there on the wall were scribblings. Hidden by the stack of mats, barely legible by the cracked paint, was a young boy's lament, crying out as to what he'd suffered at the hands of, and, yes, there was the name, *Poppy*. And beside the name Poppy was the man's real name. Reginald Henderson.

Geir and Jager turned to look at each other. Geir stepped back, pulled out his phone and took several photos. "I wonder if anybody'll take this seriously."

"It's hard to say. Let's keep looking."

Again they searched through the mats. They went gently because they weren't sure what fluids were still there after all these years. They lifted each one up and carefully examined both sides.

Between the last two mats was a small black book. Geir pulled it out and then whistled. "It's somebody's journal. Looks like a kid's handwriting."

The handwriting was childish, sometimes legible, sometimes not. There was moisture damage on it. But inside was more of what was on the wall: how Poppy had sexually abused them, how Poppy had promised them treats and alcohol and drugs in exchange for sex, and how some of the kids, this journal-writer in particular, had given Poppy whatever he wanted because he had thought Poppy cared.

By the time he'd finished reading it, Geir's heart was breaking. He shook his head and handed it to Jager. "We need to keep this safe. I doubt there are fingerprints after all this time, but it's definitely a play-by-play of everything he went through with Poppy."

"Do you think it was left here on purpose?"

Geir stared at the floor. "It blended in well. What's the chance it was lost more than anything?"

Jager opened it up. "There is a name here and a year."

"I noticed. I'm hoping, if we take that to the police, somebody will follow up on it."

"We need to know who we can take it to," Jager said. "We don't want this to get in the wrong hands."

Geir pulled out his phone and called Mason. Grateful when he answered, Geir said, "Glad I caught you. We need a cop here we can trust. Do you know one?"

"I think so," Mason said readily enough. "What did you find?"

Geir explained about the little book and the writing on the corner of the wall.

Mason's voice was sad when he said, "Unfortunately that activity is prevalent in our society. Let me look up the number for Detective Nelson." A moment later he came back and read off a number.

"I don't have a pencil, can you text that to me?"

"Will do. Give him a call and tell him what you found and where you found it."

"We have to come up with a cover story as to why we're here," Geir said with amusement in his voice. "It's hardly legal."

"Well, the door was probably unlocked, after all these years of kids busting into it, so I doubt that's an issue," Mason said, his tone neutral. "And, if you explain what you'd heard about your friend Mouse and this Poppy guy, then it doesn't take too much to understand how you found the room."

"Right." Geir stared around the room. "There's such an empty sadness here."

"Think about what those boys went through," Mason said quietly. "Chances are, whoever wrote that journal either is leading a very rough life of drugs and alcohol dependency or committed suicide or could even be living on the streets with no future because of this."

"Well, let's hope we can at least find him. Maybe the cops can get him some justice."

"How many do you think there are?" Mason asked. "If ever there was a cause I'd like to stamp out, it would be pedophiles."

"Considering what we've learned so far, I imagine he was careful with his victims. I think he knew exactly how to groom these young boys to be what he wanted. Like the journal says at one point, he gave Poppy anything he wanted because he got back love and affection and drugs," Geir said. "But once they're into that kind of a dependency trap, it's almost impossible to get out of it."

"Keep me posted. I want to know what you know," Mason said.

"Will do." Geir hung up and waited until the text came through. It was there almost instantly. He hit Dial and walked outside, wanting to put some distance between himself and what they'd found. When a man's voice answered the phone, he said, "My name is Geir Pavla. Mason told me to contact you with something we found. It's a little sensitive, and we're not exactly sure what to do with it."

"Do you want to talk over the phone, or do you want to meet in person?" the man asked. "I know Mason well. If he told you to call me, then I want to meet with you."

Geir smiled. "How about a coffee shop?"

"Where are you?"

Geir gave him the address of the school and heard the detective sigh.

"That school was one of the most run-down, troubled schools in the area. It was constantly being broken into. It was set on fire twice. It was a common drug hangout. People hated that place."

"We have a journal from somebody who was here. It's pretty rough."

CHAPTER 12

A FTER THE MEN left once again, Morning wandered into her father's rooms. She didn't know what had happened to her life, but it was no longer looking as nice as it had.

When her phone rang, she pulled it out, seeing it was her father. For the first time in a long time, she was delighted to answer the call. "Long time no hear from you," she said in a happy voice.

"Well, considering the last couple times were a little heated," her father said in a dry tone, "I figured I'd give you time to calm down."

She laughed. "Yes, you're right. I wasn't exactly easy to talk to."

There was a surprised silence, and she realized how much the last couple phone calls might have affected him.

"I'm sorry," she said quietly. "I keep forgetting to remind myself how much you did to help me over the years. I was so focused on not losing the safe haven this home was to me that, every time you brought up selling it, it terrified me."

Her father sighed, a heavy one full of a wealth of knowledge. "I know. It's one of the reasons why I dropped it for the moment. I was hoping eventually you would feel comfortable enough in the world around you that you could move. Instead it just seemed like you became more and more entrenched. Fear is a great teacher. But you still have to push it into its place so you don't stop living."

She wandered in his room as they talked. "That's very apropos right now. I'm prepping for my first-ever art gallery show and am terrified the gallery owner won't like the work I've done."

"An art gallery show?" her father asked in surprise. "I had no idea."

She chuckled. "A friend got me the showing, but I have to turn up tomorrow with some of the paintings to give him an idea of what I can do. And I'm terrified."

"And again, that's all about putting fear in its place and doing it anyway," her father said. "And, as much as I love that house you're living in, I need to move on too."

She sighed. "Do you want me to sell it?" And again she knew she'd surprised him by his startled silence.

"Are you ready to sell?" he asked cautiously.

"I'm not sure that I am," she said honestly. "But I am getting to the point where I understand why it might be necessary and why it would be the right thing to do for your sake. I know it's been my home and also my income, but, at the same time, it might be holding me back from a lot of other things."

There was approval in his voice when he said, "It sounds like you're growing up."

"Well, I am sorry it took so long," she said apologetically. She sat down on the bed and looked around at his two rooms. "The market is huge right now. I might be able to find a small house out of town and not have a mortgage."

"That would be great," he said. "I don't want you to make any decision right now. But I do need the money. I'm trying to buy property and build a house here, and of course I'd like to marry Leann."

"It's about time." Morning chuckled. "You and Leann have been together for what? Ten years?"

"Not that long. But, yeah, she said she'll make an honest man out of me." And then he chuckled loud and long.

Morning smiled. It was good to hear her father laugh. "I can always bring in a Realtor and get an estimate on what the house is worth," she said impulsively. She could feel her stomach knot at the thought. But she knew maybe it was time. "What I do know is I can't afford to buy you out, and so maybe this is the next best thing."

"The problem is, it's also your income," her father said sadly. "And that puts me in a tough position. How can a father take away his daughter's home *and* her job?"

"Well, at least I'm thinking about it and looking at options. So, if you are okay to wait a bit, give me a little more time, I'll see what I can come up with for ideas."

"Absolutely, and Leann wants to know if you'll fly over for the wedding,"

"When is it?" Her smile reached her eyes.

"September."

"Good. September, it is." She giggled. "If I can make that happen, I'll come."

"Good enough." And then her father did something he hadn't done in a long time. As he hung up, he said, "Remember, I love you."

She sat on his bed for a long moment, staring at the phone in her hand. It was a sign of how strained their relationship had been in the last year or two, since he had first brought up selling the house. It was always that big white elephant in the conversation between them. And it had set a tone that had made her worry and wonder, but, as long as she didn't have to examine it too closely, she'd been able to push it away. Now she realized how much it had affected their relationship and how opening the dialogue again had helped heal some of that.

She looked around the room, a room she rarely came into. "Why does it have to be like this?" But, of course, there was no answer.

She got up, left her father's rooms, locked them and then headed to her studio. She had a new sense of lightness in her step. A new lightness in her heart. She didn't quite understand how much change this would bring into her world, but she knew now all kinds of things were possible. But it also meant she needed to walk through the door of that gallery tomorrow. This was too important for her. Like Nancy said, it could be a great source of income.

Maybe she wouldn't have to do breakfast for strangers anymore. Not that she'd minded it, and having the house had been a great opportunity to make some money while she stayed at home and worked on her art. She stepped into the studio, put on her smock and put up a clean blank canvas. She stared at the white surface for a long moment, then shook her head and got a black canvas. She only had a couple of those.

She put it up and stared at it. "I need you to turn out as nice as the others," she said. "I feel like an idiot, but I'll offer up a prayer for it to happen anyway."

And then she grabbed her paints and started. Working from a black background forward was different, but she needed that luminescence from a night scene to come to the forefront. She didn't quite understand what she was doing until she grabbed white paint and put clouds into a night sky. And painted an early morning light breaking free over the top of them. She painted until her hand fell to her side, exhausted.

She stepped back, looked at it, but, from her extracritical eye, she couldn't see if it was any good or not. That was always an issue for her. She got too close to her work, and she couldn't figure it out. But she knew one thing: she was too tired to go on.

She put her paints back in the can, cleaned up her space, took off her smock and headed downstairs. She walked through the house, checked for messages, but nothing was on the answering machine. It had been a long time since she'd had no bookings coming in.

She had some people expected in a week or two, but business had definitely fallen off. She wasn't sure how or why, but it was a concern if she was staying because the mortgage was pretty hefty and, like her father had said, since he'd cosigned for her, he also carried a portion of the debt.

Walking into the kitchen, she put on a pot of coffee and headed to the fridge to look for food. She pulled out her phone and texted Geir, asking if he was coming for dinner.

"Yes," Geir answered. "Be there in about two hours."

She checked the clock, realizing that would put them home at about six. She looked through the freezer for something to cook and found some of her favorite pasta sauce she had frozen. She pulled it out, estimated the amount of sauce, and put on her pasta pot full of water. Once it boiled, she threw in lasagna noodles. Now with the sauce warming while the lasagna noodles cooked, she prepped salamis, brought out the cottage cheese and started grating mozzarella. It only took twenty minutes to throw the whole thing together.

Before long she sprinkled the last of the grated cheese over the top, putting the whole thing in the oven. She still had some romaine lettuce, so she would make a Caesar salad to go with that. She did all the prep work except for the dressing and set it off to one side, waiting for the casserole to cook.

In the meantime, she headed to her office to tackle some paperwork.

When the landline phone in the office rang, she answered it automatically. Nobody was on the other end. She hung up and went back to her paperwork. But it rang again a few minutes later. She picked it up and said, "Hello?"

No answer.

The next time she answered, "This is Blossom's Bed-and-Breakfast." When again there was no answer, she asked, "Is this a wrong number?" She thought she could hear heavy breathing but didn't know what that was all about. She hung up.

When it rang a fourth time, she picked it up in exasperation and said, "Morning Blossom's Bed-and-Breakfast. How can I help you?"

"You can't." A male voice laughed. "Did you like the mouse?" And then the phone went dead.

She dropped the receiver onto the desktop, staring at it like an asp about to strike her. She could feel herself hyperventilating. Finally she pulled out her cell phone and called Geir. Again she didn't question why she was calling him.

"Are we late?" Geir asked in a teasing voice.

"A man just called," she said in a rush. "He said something about me not being able to help him and then asked if I liked the mouse."

Geir was silent on the other end, and she could feel her

heart willing him to tell her it would be okay, that all this would go away and that her life would return to normal.

And then he said, "Are you inside?"

"I am."

"Are you alone?"

"Yes, I am. Why?" She walked to the front door. "I'm now standing at the front door."

"Make sure you have locked the doors. All of them."

"Damn it, Geir. What does this mean?"

"It means, you've been caught up in this web of deceit and lies that I'm in." His voice was tired and filled with sorrow. "I'm so sorry."

"Are you sure? Maybe it's something else." Panicked, she raced to the kitchen door. "Okay, the front and back doors are locked."

"And now I want you to carefully go to all the French doors on that bottom floor, like your father's, then go up to your studio and make sure all the French doors are closed and locked."

"What about your room and Jager's room?"

"One at a time, systematically lock all those doors. Do you hear me?"

"I'm back in my father's room." She walked to the French doors. And she stopped. "I can't lock it," she cried out in the panic.

"Why not?"

"It's broken. Where are you? I want you home now."

"We're on the way. Just hang tight. We'll be there in ten minutes."

"Ten minutes might not be fast enough," she said in a dark voice.

"Go up to your room and lock yourself in. Stay there

until we get there." And he hung up.

She poured herself a cup of coffee, though she didn't need the caffeine, considering how hard it was to hold the cup steady, and went to the back staircase and up to her room. But, instead of going to her room, she went to her studio. There she sat down on the overstuffed broken-down chair she kept in there beside the futon. The French doors were open still because of the paint smell. She walked onto the small balcony and stared at her backyard. She hated this. She hated that she didn't know what the hell she was supposed to do with this darkness, this evil. She shook her head at the term. "Why is this all happening?" But there was no answer to be found in her backyard.

Thankfully nobody was skulking around. She didn't remember when she'd last checked that lock on her father's door, but she'd closed it recently, or had she? She cast her mind back, but she couldn't count on it. It was hard to know exactly what had happened when the days were just a blur.

Part of that was her painting. She'd become so unfocused, or so focused, on her painting that she'd lost track of everything going on around her. And that meant there was a good chance she wouldn't have heard anybody coming in. She had always left the front door unlocked, but the bells let her know when somebody entered. And that was when she realized that maybe, just maybe, the bells weren't working. How could she check for sure? She grabbed her phone and called Nancy. "Are you at home?"

"I just got in," her friend said, sounding tired, her breath coming in puffs.

"Are you okay?"

"Yeah, I just unloaded the groceries. Why?"

"I got a weird phone call today, and I'm kind of un-

GEIR

nerved by it," Morning admitted.

"Do you want me to come over?" Nancy asked. "I'm tired, but, hell, you're just across the street, so it's not a biggie."

It was on the edge of her tongue to say, yes, and then she realized that, if something were going on here, she would be putting Nancy in danger. Morning took a deep breath and let it out slowly. "Nah, it's okay. I don't want to put you out. The guys will be here any minute anyway."

"Okay, if you're sure?" she answered. "I don't mind."

"No, that's okay. Did you have a good day?"

"Good enough," Nancy said. "I did hear back from one of the jobs I applied for."

"Awesome! Where is it?"

Nancy answered a bit cautiously, "New Mexico. Albuquerque, New Mexico."

Morning sighed. "That sounds lovely. I sure hate to lose you."

"Come with me," Nancy said. "God knows I don't want to move alone."

"I don't know that I'm ready for something like that yet," Morning said. "I talked to my dad today. And he's delighted I'm thinking about selling."

"Are you?"

Morning looked around her studio, thought about everything that had happened in the last few days and how it was letting her drop many of the ties she'd hung on to for so long, ties she'd held so tightly because she was afraid to end up in the situation she'd started out in. "Yes. Finally. And my dad does need the money. I'm not sure exactly where I got the idea it was an option to not sell. I've been a very selfish daughter."

"Well, don't do anything too rash," Nancy warned. "You do have some time yet."

"I do have some time, though I'm not sure how much. He's getting married again."

"Oh, wow! To Leann?"

Morning chuckled. "Yes, to Leann. And it's about time."

"Where are they getting married?"

"In Switzerland. In September. I've been invited to the wedding."

"That's a nice olive branch," Nancy said. "It's time."

After Morning hung up, she sat there on the broken-down chair, staring at the paintings. All of a sudden she saw the one she'd been working on—really saw it this time—seeing how the light, the cream, and the white moved through the clouds, as if something almost mystical was behind it. And she realized Nancy was right. Out loud to the empty room, she said, "Yes. It's time."

THE MEN BOLTED from the Jeep and raced to the front door. It was locked. They hit the doorbell several times and waited.

"I told her to lock herself into her room," Geir said, pulling out his phone. He called her. He couldn't even begin to express the relief that washed through him when he heard her voice. "We're at the front door."

"Really? Did you ring the doorbell?"

"Yeah. Hang on a sec." He pushed the button several times.

"I'm coming down."

He looked at Jager. "Her doorbell may have been disconnected inside the house."

Jager's gaze hardened. "Sounds like we should be standing watch tonight."

"I hate to, I do. I don't want to terrify her any more than she already is."

Just then the door opened in front of them. But no bells went off. She smiled, hit the doorbell, and, sure enough, she couldn't hear it right here on the front step. She shook her head. "I think somebody has tampered with my doorbell and the bells that go off when somebody comes in."

"I'll check it out," Jager said.

"Was there some mention of dinner?" Geir asked in a gentle voice, steering her toward the kitchen. He didn't want her to get more concerned, and he knew Jager would easily find out the source of the problem. In Geir's mind, he figured it had been cut either upstairs or in the office.

Morning obviously knew what he was doing because she tossed him a fulminating look. "Don't try to hide anything from me."

He shook his head and laughed. "Wouldn't dream of it."

She rolled her eyes. "Lucky for you, I have to check the oven anyway." She put on oven mitts and opened the oven door, pulling out a bubbling hot lasagna.

Geir stared at it in awe. "Now that's a work of art."

She placed it on top of the stove, turned off the oven, tossed down the oven mitts and grabbed a big wooden board. "Only for a hungry man." Then she put on her oven mitts again, grabbed the lasagna and placed it on the board.

When he saw the Caesar salad, he asked, "Is there anything I can do to help?"

"You're on the side where the dishes are. Bring out enough for the three of us."

"Did you ever hear from the other couple?"

She looked up and smiled. "They phoned. They got an emergency call. They couldn't find me, as I was in the studio. Anyway, they packed up and left this morning, went straight to the airport. He said to go ahead and charge their credit card for the extra night."

Jager grinned. "At least they called."

She shrugged. "The thing is, people travel. And when you leave home, things can happen. It's fine. I'm not out money. At least they did the right thing."

He gave that one to her. "Good point. What are there, ten million people here?" he joked. "I swear to God they were all out driving on the roads today."

She chuckled. "Right?"

Just then Jager walked in. He took one look at the lasagna and whistled. "Man, am I ever glad we stayed here."

"Yeah, well, I don't normally do meals, remember? Just breakfast. Hence the name, bed-and-*breakfast*."

"Sure, but, now that I know, anytime I'm in San Diego, I definitely want to stay here."

She smiled. "Thank you, that's very nice."

She served up dinner for the three of them, giving the men each a piece twice as big as her own, and then motioned toward the Caesar salad she had mixed up with dressing and parmesan. "Dig in. As you can see, there's lots."

It took them a bit to get through the plate of hot bubbling lasagna, but Geir had to admit it was well worth taking the time.

When he was almost done, she asked, "Did you find anything at the hideaway?"

Geir nodded and explained about the message on the wall and the journal. "We did call the cops, and we did meet with the detective. That's where we were when you called me."

She sighed. "The world really sucks, doesn't it?"

"It does sometimes, yes," Geir said. "But right now, we're inside. We're safe. We have a hot meal. That's more than a lot of folks have."

She nodded.

As soon as they were finished, Geir and Jager got up to do dishes, and Morning put on the teakettle, bringing out leftover mini-cheesecakes.

Geir eyed them and, with a happy sigh, said, "Oh, yum."

She chuckled. "They're easy to keep around, and they'll last for a week."

"Not when we're here," Jager said, grabbing one with a big smile.

As they sat down again, she turned to Geir. "So, what's next?"

He sighed. "We'll have four-hour watches through the night and see if your tormentor comes back."

She drummed her fingers on the tabletop as she watched and waited, as if thinking heavily about his proposition. "When are you two planning on leaving?"

"We've made progress. If we can nail Poppy, then we'll be very happy. But, if we can't, I'm not sure how long we're staying."

"Mason said three nights. Tonight is the third."

Both men nodded. "It's possible we'll stay a fourth night." Geir knew what she would say. "You're right. That's not any comfort, knowing we won't be here to protect you."

She looked up, smiled at him and said, "Then you'll just have to solve this problem before you leave, won't you?"

Geir snorted. She had completely surprised him.

She stood, scooped up their small cheesecake dishes, rinsed them and loaded them in the dishwasher. "I have some office work to do. If you need me, I'll be in there." She turned and walked away.

Geir stared at Jager. "She's taking it better than I thought she would."

Jager shook his head. "Or it hasn't set in yet. Or maybe it's set in, but she hasn't quite figured out how it pertains to her. Or she has a very cool, controlled exterior, and right now she's bawling her eyes out in the office."

At that, Geir stared at Jager. "Is that likely?" Straining his ear, he heard something in the distance. His shoulders sagged. "Yes, that's exactly what she's doing." He got up and said, "Back soon."

Jager chuckled. "Yeah, sure you will."

Geir gave him a hard look. "What does that mean?"

"It means, you're already a goner, and you don't even know it. RIP."

Geir stared at him for a moment as he considered Jager's words. "Long-distance relationships don't work."

"Then maybe you should know what Nancy told me. When I took her home, she mentioned that Morning and her father both own the house and he's been trying to get her to sell it for a while. He needs his money, and Nancy doesn't think it's a good place for her."

"Why not?"

"Something to do with being too safe."

Geir thought about that as he walked toward the office. This house wasn't as safe anymore. He entered her office to find her face buried in her hands, the lights off, as she stood beside her desk. No way he could do anything but walk over and wrap his arms around her and hold her close.

CHAPTER 13

MORNING DIDN'T EVEN cry. She just burrowed deep into the caring arms and let Geir hold her. She'd been independent, standing on her own two feet for a long time now. At least she thought she had been, but she'd been hiding behind the safety of her house, getting through life relatively easily with an income from property she only half owned while she dabbled but didn't really focus on her art.

Now everything was changing. It wasn't that she was scared of change, but it was unnerving to say the least. And this nightmare was incredibly disturbing. She wasn't even sure she could sleep tonight.

Or sleep ever again, considering somebody had been in the bedrooms messing them up. And for what? For a lark, just to terrorize her? She didn't understand, neither did she understand the mind-set of anybody who would do that.

Finally she let out a heavy sigh and tried to step away. But he wouldn't let her. Instead his arms tugged her back, up against him, and he held her close. With his head resting on top of hers, they just stood together like that.

"I can stand on my own, you know," she muttered.

"Maybe I can't," he said quietly. "You have to understand I never would have put you in danger if I had known."

"I don't think you did it on purpose," she exclaimed, pulling her head back so she could look up at him. "That's not what this is about. It's just scary to see the safety of my world fracture. It wasn't even a real world. I was like someone living in one of those snow globes, content to live inside and just touch the world through my guests, and I didn't have to have a real job. I didn't have to focus on my art. I had this wonderful gift of a place to stay. Instead of being grateful for it, I let the opportunity slide away."

She could see confusion in his gaze. She quickly explained the situation with her father. "I spoke with him today," she admitted. "And told him that I was finally able to see how unfair I'd been."

Geir nodded and smiled. "I'm sure he was happy to hear that."

"If he had lots of money, it wouldn't be an issue, but it's not fair that, when he doesn't have the money, I'm sitting on his full asset base. Worse, I use the money from the guests to pay my mortgage and to live."

This time, when she pulled back, he let her go. She was almost sorry to leave his arms because it had been very reassuring and comforting being held by him. She collapsed into her chair and stared up at him. "It's just everything was happening at once. It started with my artwork, I think. I don't know. It feels like my world's splitting wide open."

"Maybe instead of thinking of this as tearing apart your world, you should consider it as being a cocoon whose time has come to open."

She stared at him for a long moment, then gave him a wry smile. "I thought I was supposed to be the happy, upbeat person."

He grinned. "You are. But everybody comes under some stress, and when Mother Nature or the universe or God, whatever you want to call it, throws your life into a tailspin like this, the stress is amplified. You've got not only your foundation—which is your home and money, your income—at stake, but, all of a sudden, you also have that core of who you really want to be, your artistic talent, coming under stress."

"Now my own personal safety," she muttered. She turned and looked around the office, seeing the years she'd sat here working away and yet not understanding or seeing or acknowledging there had to be an end. It wasn't like she had won a lottery and could afford to pay her father back nor was it like she had the money to pay out half a million dollars for his share. Property prices being what they were, she knew it would be at least that much.

A second heavy sigh eased up from her deep inner valley through her chest and out her lips. She collapsed back in her chair and said, "I'm not normally somebody who is afraid, but this is definitely an experience I'm not all that comfortable with."

"If you did sell the house, what would you do?"

She shook her head. "I have no idea. Because, if I sell, it's also my job, my income."

He nodded. "You could always buy another bed-and-breakfast, though it wouldn't be here. It would have to be someplace outside of San Diego, where the prices are a whole lot less." He chuckled. "If your place is worth a million dollars, no way I can afford to move here."

She nodded. "Right. But it's the location. It's the size. The fact that it's already an operating business." She raised both hands in mock surrender. "I guess I'm selling the business too. Even the name of the business?" She shook her head. "I don't even know how to answer the question of where I would move and what I would do. This is all new to me. I just don't know."

He nodded. "So maybe today isn't the day to worry about it. You've started the process. Let your body and your mind and your world come to terms with it, and see what pops up in the morning." He leaned forward. "Did you paint again today?"

She nodded. "But it's different." She wrinkled up her nose. "It's really different."

He held out his hand to her. "Show me," he said in a commanding tone.

"Well, since you've already seen the others ..."

She put her hand in his, letting him tug her against his side, wrapping an arm around her shoulders. The two walked up the stairs, comfortable, no pressure, just a strong sense of friendship. *No, not friendship.* Her mind rejected that. There was so much more here than friendship. "Are you married?"

He glanced down at her, a silvery light in his gaze. "No, I'm not."

"How come?"

"Because I saw so many rough marriages when I was in the navy that I swore I'd never do that to another woman."

"Another woman?"

"Some of my best friends broke up with their wives. The problem was, I knew several of the wives. I was good friends with them. And I saw how much the navy lifestyle tortured them. Not everybody is happy to see their man go off to war or out to sea, never knowing if they will be coming back."

She nodded. "Same for all military wives. I imagine anybody in the service goes through the same thing."

"And divorce rates are very high," he added.

"To be expected." Upstairs on the landing, she walked

forward and unlocked her studio.

He stood at the doorway. "Do I have to close my eyes again?" he joked.

She smiled and nodded. "You so do." She grabbed his hand. "Close them now, and I'll put you in position."

Obediently he snapped them closed, and she walked him to where he would be standing in front of the easel.

"Now you can look."

He opened his eyes. A surprised look came across his face. "Wow. That's really different."

She wasn't sure what the word *different* meant this time coming from him. It was the word she'd used, but that didn't mean she understood how he had applied it in this circumstance.

"But it's good." His words came slowly. "It's more than good." He shook his head. "You've painted four very different paintings. The scope of how you're utilizing this light is fantastic."

"Well, tomorrow is Friday, so we'll see what the gallery owner thinks about it."

Again that silvery gaze slanted her way. "Are you nervous about it?"

"Very."

"What time is your appointment?"

"Ten in the morning. I'd normally make it midafternoon, but as Nancy is around to help out most of the time if I have to leave, I was good with it." She absentmindedly studied the painting. "After all, I wasn't about to say no. Although I'm so nervous I'm not sure if I will last that long."

He chuckled. "I'll make sure you get there on time."

"By then I'll be a basket of nerves," she complained good-naturedly.

He glanced around the room. "This is a nice space for you."

She nodded. "Technically it was another bedroom. But I needed a studio so ..." Morning studied her room in the half-light. "I need a couple more hours to finish the black painting." She sat her fisted hands on her hips and tapped her toe on the floor as she considered the lighting issue. "Because it's a night scene, I wonder if I could get away with working on it in this light."

"We can pull in a couple extra lamps if you need them," Geir said.

She looked at him in surprise, happy to see he understood her artistic point of view. "Thank you."

He disappeared around the corner and brought back two pole lamps, the ones she kept by her couch in her bedroom.

She stared at them. "How did you know they were in there?"

"I didn't." He grinned. "I just went in to see what you did have and thought these would do it."

He set them up on either side of the canvas, tilted the heads of the lamps and turned them on. Light filled the room. It wasn't the same as the preferred natural sunlight, but it wasn't half bad. In fact, it made some of her mistakes a little more glaringly obvious.

She shook her head. "I should have thought of that. I definitely see some areas I have to work on."

"Good. I'll go grab my laptop."

She shifted to stare at him. "Why?"

"Because I'll sit in that chair over there and work while you paint."

Her stomach got queasy. She dropped her gaze to the floor. "I haven't ever painted while somebody watched

GEIR

before."

"Well, there's a first time for everything," he said gently. "Besides, it's not like I'll be watching you. I'll be working on the laptop."

She thought about it, then took a deep breath. "Fine. But if you stop me from being able to paint as I need to, I'll have to ask you to leave."

"If that's the case, I'll sit out in the hall."

She glanced down the hallway to see the corner of a chair between all the bedrooms. "That would work."

He disappeared.

She threw on her smock and grabbed one of her paintbrushes, walked back to the painting and studied it. She could see a couple places that needed work, but what else was she planning on doing to this painting? Always before, she'd painted and then suddenly knew when it was done. "I guess I have to trust it to be the same this time."

She walked back to her pots of paints, grabbed her palette and picked up the colors, mixing them as she needed. Stepping back toward the canvas, she let her brush drift gently across the sky. And with that first stroke, she was transported once again into the world of her own creation as she gently smudged and smoothed, stroked and highlighted the canvas in front of her. She stepped back at one point, frowned, reached for a different color and resumed her work.

When she did that again, she wasn't sure. She looked at it for the longest time. In her mind, she asked the question, *Am I done? Is there anything else I need to do for this one?*

No came the answer within her mind.

She smiled. "I think that's it."

Geir stood.

She glanced at him and frowned. "I forgot you were

here. I hope you weren't watching me."

"Self-conscious, are you?" But he walked toward her with a smile on his face. "Don't worry about it. I was working on my laptop."

She sighed with relief. "That's good because, for all I know, I might do something weird while I'm painting. Like hold my tongue sideways or something."

He chuckled. "From the few glances I caught when I looked up, you looked perfectly normal."

She grinned and stepped back. He walked around farther back from the painting than she was, so he could get a full view. She heard a soft, gentle sigh escape his lips.

He whispered, "Perfect."

And her heart swelled. She turned and grinned up at him. "Really?"

He nodded. "Really. You're incredibly talented."

Self-consciousness hitting her again, she walked to the sink and washed her brushes, palette and then her hands. She gently removed the smock from her clothing. As she turned to face Geir, he reached around her and grabbed a piece of paper towel off the roll.

"Hold still." He brushed paint off her cheek.

When he held out the paper towel, she could see a bit of gentle blue. She chuckled. "Of course. No way would I get away from that scot-free, would I?"

He tossed the paper towel on the counter. "What do you need for this to be ready to go?"

She looked at it, sniffed the air, walked to the French doors and opened them. "It needs air in here. The painting needs to dry, and the best way is if there is circulating air. Plus the room stinks of paint."

He stood at her side as they stared out into the evening

air. "I just don't like to leave the doors open." His voice held his concern.

She slid her gaze at him sideways. "I often do."

He drew his brows together and glared at her. "Remember how we're back to the fact you need to change the way you do things?"

"How else am I supposed to get my paintings to dry?"

He turned to study each of the paintings. "I'm not sure what is the best thing. I'll have to research that to find out, but leaving your doors open, particularly after several break-ins, is not ideal."

She nodded. "I get that. But tomorrow is very important to me."

He nodded. "In that case, I'll stay here in the studio. You're right beside me in the bedroom there, so I can keep an eye on your place too."

She stared at him in surprise. "Why would you do that?"

"To make sure nobody comes in the studio and accidentally, or on purpose, damages your paintings."

She stared at him in horror. "They wouldn't …" Her frown deepened. "Would they?"

He nodded. "I can't say for sure they would," he cautioned, "but it's hard to say what's on somebody's mind. Look at the bedrooms that have been tossed. How easy would it be to splash paint on these so they're ruined forever?"

She wrapped her arms around her stomach. "Okay, that's almost enough to make me physically ill." She stared at the paintings. "Where can I keep them so they'll be safe?"

He walked toward several older paintings stacked on the wall, crouching in front of them. "Your paintings, can they be moved?"

She nodded. "I would wrap them in cotton before I took them down, but, for the moment, they just need to be someplace safe."

"Do you have a closet big enough?"

She shook her head. "No, I don't."

"Well, that goes back to me staying here in this room then because now it's not just you but also your work that needs to be protected."

She wasn't sure what to think of him. She'd never had anybody make an offer like that before. "Why would you do that?"

One eyebrow rose. "Because I'm a nice guy?"

"Because you'd feel guilty if anything happened to them," she corrected.

He chuckled. "True. But that still doesn't change the fact you need these paintings in this wonderful condition so you can take them to the gallery in the morning, correct?"

She nodded and sighed. "Correct."

"In that case, you head off to bed, and I'll do my first shift sitting here. When Jager and I switch, I'll make sure he knows the scoop and comes up here."

She smiled. "Are you going back to your bed to sleep? I don't want to think of you sitting up here half the night."

"Jager and I are doing four-hour shifts. He's sleeping right now."

She glanced at the door. "I never even thought about where he was." She shook her head. "But it seems like, when I'm painting lately, I completely lose myself in it."

"Is that not the way it's always been?" He was curious.

"No, not at all. It's nothing I've experienced before. Not until I did these new paintings."

He nodded. "Interesting."

"I don't know about *interesting*, but *weird* will do." She walked to the door, cast a saucy glance back at him and said, "Good night, dear knight."

At that, his eyebrows shot upward, and she chuckled. "Obviously you're a knight in shining armor if you're standing guard over me and my paintings for the evening."

He grinned. "In that case, do I get a kiss as a thank-you?"

"In that case, you get it in the morning," she said, waving at him as she walked out of the room.

His laughter followed her. She walked into her bedroom and realized she didn't have the two lamps by the couch, but they weren't required for tonight. It was already quite late. She glanced at the clock. It was past eleven.

She walked into the bathroom, took a quick shower because she generally had paint in her hair by the time she was done with a late session. When she was done, she dried off and stepped out of the bathroom. She threw on a camisole and boy shorts in soft cotton and went to her bed.

With her hair twisted up in a bun, she lay down and almost immediately fell asleep.

She swore it was only a few minutes later when she woke up. She thought she heard somebody outside her room. She smiled, realizing it would be Geir. She wanted to call out to him but figured that would just be an invitation, and he'd take it a different way than she meant it.

The trouble was, as she lay here thinking about the way he would take it, she realized just how interested she was. And, if he was leaving the next day, she didn't have much time in order to show him that kind of interest.

She lay here wondering what she would do.

Then her gaze caught the clock, and she saw it was nearly three o'clock in the morning. It was probably the changing of the guard, and Jager would come to her studio. She flopped onto her back, considering the two men who would do such a thing. Sure, they were worried about somebody coming back into the house, but they also knew how important those paintings were to her.

She flipped over again and groaned. "No way I'll sleep now," she grumbled. She heard footsteps again. She froze. Had he heard her?

"Are you okay?" Geir asked in a low whisper from the hallway.

She hopped out of bed, ran to the door and opened it a crack. "I'm fine. How come you're still walking around? Shouldn't you be in bed?"

His eyes gleamed with silvery light as he stared at her body. And she realized how little she wore. She closed the door slightly. But he slowly raised that gaze to lock onto hers.

"I was just heading to bed." His voice was husky, deep. But he didn't move.

And neither did she. Her breath caught in the back of her throat as she warred with herself about what she wanted. She knew exactly what Nancy would say. *Seize the moment and charge full speed ahead.*

"ARE YOU GOING to let me in?" His voice had deepened to a grittiness level. He knew he sounded hoarse. The heat rolling through him threatened to take over. The sight of her in that skimpy top, her breasts plump, filling out that top, her nipples reaching for him, and the shadow showing through the bottoms, ... it was too much.

He closed his eyes and stood there, fisting his hands. "Sorry," he said as he struggled for control. "But you are something else."

He felt rather than heard her reaction. He opened his eyes to see her standing there, curious, interested, hesitant. But he didn't want her questioning the way she felt. He wanted her to throw herself in his arms and to feel exactly the same way he did. Because, right now, all he wanted to do was throw her to the floor and ravage her. But in a good way.

He ordered his body to move, to walk down the hall, to go past her room. But his body refused to listen. It had a mind of its own, and already his groin was seriously tight. He again closed his eyes, adding in a deep breath, letting it out slowly, then repeating it again. Just when he thought he would be okay, that he could get past this without an incredibly humiliating moment he hadn't had since he was fourteen, he felt her hand on his chest. His breath sucked in, and he opened his eyes to stare at her.

"Don't tease," he said, his voice hard. "I'm too close to the edge."

"I can see that," she whispered. "And there's something so fascinating about thinking you're feeling that way about me."

He shook his head. "Surely you know how incredibly sexy you are."

She smiled mistily up at him. "No, I'm not so sure I do." Her other hand slid over his belly, up his chest, until both were around his neck. She lifted herself on her tiptoes, her lips almost level with his.

His heart raced. He gripped the doorknob with his iron fist, desperate to hold back. He wasn't sure where she was going with this, but he hoped, dear God, he hoped.

She slid her fingers through his hair and whispered, "Why don't you show me?"

And that was all it took. He wrapped her tight in his arms, crushing her against him, his lips hard on hers. He heard the startled squeak from behind her lips, but he didn't dare let her go. He deepened the kiss, showing her exactly how he felt about her. His arm stroked the full length of her body, reaching down to cup her cheeks. He hitched her higher, wrapping her legs around his waist until he carried her. His leg was sore as hell from all his earlier activities today, but he wouldn't acknowledge it. It had been a problem for two years. He wasn't about to start coddling it now.

He gently closed the door, one arm under her ass, holding her tight, and carried her to the bed.

She looked at him, her eyes deeper than midnight as she watched in wonder. "I've never been carried before."

He brushed a kiss against her lips, then gently lowered her to the blankets, following her down.

He led her into the riotous desire ripping through him. He had her stripped of her camisole in seconds. He was feasting on her nipples that had teased and tortured him since he'd first caught sight of them, loose and shimmying against the camisole material.

She moaned and twisted gently in his arms. Her fingers stroked his hair, holding him close against her. "Oh, my God," she whispered, "that feels so wonderful."

He sucked harder and deeper, her back arching, a moan escaping. He slipped fingers into her panties, pulling them off, tossing them to the floor. He stroked the fleshy lips, feeling the moisture already at the heart of her. Dipping his fingers inside, he stroked, caressed, her body writhing beneath him, and still he wouldn't let up.

She cried out, "Geir, I want you now."

But he wouldn't stop. He shifted his attention to her other breast, caressing the nipple with as much love and care as he had the first one, before taking it into his mouth and sucking it in a deep pulsing rhythm. At the same time, he slid his fingers deeper inside her and stroked over and over.

Her body wept with joy; she arched as her climax ripped through her until she lay shuddering on the bed.

Just as she was about to speak, he crushed her lips, his tongue sliding inside, dueling with hers, not giving her a respite or time to relax and enjoy. Instead, he spread her legs as wide as he could. Just for the moment, resting at the heart of her, he lifted his head up and looked down at her.

She smiled, wrapped her arms trustingly around his neck and whispered, "Yes."

And he plunged deep. She cried out, her body arching at the forceful possession. But it was how he felt. She was his. She always would be.

A primitive need drove him as he pounded into her. She was small, not delicate, but not a huge bold woman either, and he needed to be careful, but it was so damn hard. He didn't want to hurt her, but, at the same time, his body had taken over, and his passion ripped through him as he drove her closer and closer to the edge again.

When she gave a muffled scream and flew off the edge, he followed her with a deep guttural groan and slid down beside her. She lay quivering in his arms, the aftershocks still moving through her body. He smiled, but it was all he could do. He was exhausted, his body expending so much energy to hold back that passion. When finally he'd unleashed it, his own climax had been earth-shattering. He tried to catch his breath as he lay here.

Finally she rolled over and looked at him. "Oh, my God."

He stared at her lazily, reached over and kissed her gently. "What does that mean?"

She gave him the sweetest smile. "It means, I'm so grateful I opened my bedroom door tonight."

CHAPTER 14

A ND MORNING WASN'T lying. That had been the most earth-shattering sex she had ever participated in. She had no idea passion could rage like that. But, from the minute she'd seen his physical reaction, she'd wanted to know what that kind of passionate power was like. What it was like to have somebody want her as desperately as he did at the moment. And it had been worth everything.

Her fingers stroked his arm, his side, his back. He stilled. She frowned, leaned up on her elbow, pulled his arm up and rolled him slightly toward her so she could look at his back. She cried out softly at the scars. She stroked across the mangled one over his shoulder blade and several more on his spine.

When she came to his buttocks, there were scars, big ugly scars across his flesh. There was a huge indentation on the top of his right buttock, damage from whatever injury had befallen him.

She stroked her fingers along and out and around, but that wasn't enough. She sat up and kissed every spot she could find.

Slowly he relaxed as if he'd thought she would run from him, run from seeing the scars of a body that had been ravaged by something terrible.

When she'd finally explored all of his back, his thighs,

and came to the prosthetic of his lower right leg, she stopped and stared. Her fingers gently stroked along the edge where the cup held his lower leg in place.

He stiffened, waiting to see what she'd do, only to feel his heart ease as she dropped a kiss onto his knee and said, "I didn't even notice."

"Good," he whispered. "I didn't want you to think less of me. Serving my country took a toll on my body."

She looked up at him. "How could anybody think less of you for what you've been through? You served our country, for all of us, and this is what happens to you? If anything, I want to murder the person who did this to you."

"What makes you think a person did this?" he asked curiously.

She shook her head. "I have no idea." Her hands stroked his other leg, his foot—a foot that had to be at least twice the size hers. With a smile, she stretched out her leg, held her foot against his and shook her head. "You're just so damn big." She stroked her leg up his thigh and his hips as he chuckled.

And she saw scars on the top of his thighs, and an old scar against the inside of his hip. She figured it had something to do with internal injuries. But definitely nothing was wrong with his manhood. It rose proud and strong in front of her again. She stared at it, her fingers stroking over the top and back again as it waved. He groaned, and she closed her fingers tightly around it, sliding up and down and then up again.

He shuddered. His body open and available. He was such a big man and so accepting of anything she wanted to do for him.

She sighed with happiness, gently cupping the globes

GEIR

between his thighs and kissed the head in front of her.

His good hand gently grasped her hair, and he whispered, "Too much of that and I won't be able to hold back."

"I've already seen how much control you have." Her fingers gently slid across the top again. "And it's a lot."

He chuckled. "That was not control. I took one look at you, and my body reacted."

She chuckled and rose on her knees, gently straddling his hips. Instead of letting him enter her again, she gently slid up and down the length of him.

He sighed, his hands coming to rest on her thighs. "It's been a long time," he admitted quietly.

"Good," she whispered. "I'd hate to think you spread this beautiful body around. So many wouldn't appreciate it."

He chuckled. "I don't think *appreciation* is what most people think when they see this body."

She flicked her tongue across his nipples and gently nipped one. A rumble rolled up his chest, and he hugged her close. She lay against him, wondering about what had happened to this beautiful man. At the same time, she knew it would bring him pain and sorrow to ask, and she didn't want anything taking from their joy of the moment.

She rose high, and, this time when she sat, she slid down over his shaft until she was fully seated. She threw her head back, eyes closed. She reached out her hands for him to grab as she said, "You know what I always dreamed about?"

"What?" he asked, his voice thick, hoarse.

"Riding." And she started to ride.

She woke hours later, her body sore, achy, thrumming with pleasure, even hours after their last lovemaking session. She wrapped her arms around the big man beside her, loving when he tugged her closer. "I don't want this night to end," she whispered.

He dropped a kiss on her temple. "Neither do I."

She sighed with happiness and just lay here awash in the peace and quiet and the joy of the moment.

A phone buzzed somewhere next to them. Geir made to move, and she moaned in protest. "I have to check it," he whispered gently, easing out of her arms.

She watched as he picked up his pants and snatched his phone from the pocket.

As soon as he read the message, he bolted to his feet, jumped into his boxers and jeans and pulled his T-shirt over his head. He raced to the door, turned to look back at her, held a finger to his lips and whispered, "Stay here." And he ran out into the hall.

She sat up, realizing the call must have come from Jager. Desperate to not end up nude in the middle of a gunfight, or whatever kind of fight this would be, she quickly dressed in yoga pants and a sports bra and sat cross-legged on the bed, waiting for one of them to let her know everything was all right. She kept the light off, sitting in the silent dark.

JAGER'S MESSAGE HAD been clear. One word: **Trouble**.

Geir slid along the hall toward the studio. The door was open. He peered in. Jager stood beside the French doors.

In a low whisper he said, "Someone came through the backyard and into the house through the French doors of her father's rooms."

Geir's jaw hardened. "Good. Now let's get the bastard." Geir went down the back stairway while Jager made his way to the front stairway. Creeping as quietly as he could by putting most his weight on the banisters, off the creaky stairs of an old house, Geir made his way to the bottom and stopped. Somewhere this guy was hiding, and it appeared he'd been in the house enough times that he knew the nooks and crannies, the best places to be. Mentally Geir shifted through the various rooms, wondering where the intruder was going and what he was after.

Just then he heard the sound of papers shuffling in the office. Not understanding what could possibly be of interest there, but knowing Jager was coming down that hallway, Geir slid into her father's bedroom to see if it was just one intruder or two. Nobody hid in the bedroom. Geir slid back out again, down the hallway toward the office. Still he heard sounds of papers being moved, and he knew Jager would hear it too.

As he came up to the corner and peered around to the office door, he saw Jager holding up a single finger to say one man inside. Perfect. As one they stepped into the room, and Jager said, "Just what do you think you're doing?"

The intruder froze.

Geir flicked on the light, and his eyebrows shot up. "What the hell?"

Ken glared back at him. "What are you two doing down here? Did you break curfew?"

Jager shook his head. "Hardly. I watched you come across the backyard and break into the downstairs room."

Ken shook his head. "Like hell," he scoffed.

Geir motioned at the paperwork. "What are you doing here?"

He shrugged. "I was looking for something."

"Oh, yeah?" Morning said from behind them.

Geir turned and stared at her. "I told you to stay up-

DALE MAYER

stairs," he snapped.

She nodded. She held the mouse in her hand. "Is this what you're looking for?"

Geir watched as Ken's gaze locked on it. He frowned, gripped the reservations book and a credit card slip, then said, "I'll take that too."

"Why is that?"

"I don't care why it is," Ken said. "I'm being paid to pick it up, so I don't give a shit about the reasons behind it."

"And is the man who hired you driving your getaway vehicle?"

Ken stared at him. "What do you know about a getaway vehicle?"

"Poppy put you up to this?"

Ken froze. "Poppy?"

Jager smiled. "Does that name get to you? Are you one of his little boys?"

The man sneered. "Like hell. No way somebody would do that to me."

"So why are you here?" Morning snapped. "Why didn't he show up himself?"

And that's when a new voice entered the discussion. "He did." The voice was gravelly behind them.

Suddenly Morning was thrust into the room, and the second man entered, only this one held a handgun.

He stared at Ken and sneered. "You couldn't even retrieve the damn stuffed mouse. You're the one who placed it here, and you couldn't even find it again. That's what I get for picking a wannabe. But you were the only local I could get on short notice."

Ken stared back at him. "What the hell? You sent me in here to do the job. You should have just left me to do it." He waved at the gun. "That'll only make things worse."

The stranger stood beside them. Geir took a quick look, noticing his features. He was a man in his mid- to late sixties, big, but almost Santa-friendly looking until he smiled. A nasty little smile. He wondered if Ken had any idea just how dangerous Poppy was.

"Poppy, I presume?" Geir asked. He heard Morning's gasp of shock.

She turned to look at him. "It is you."

He looked at her in surprise. "Do you know me?"

She nodded. "I used to live in the house across the street from your house."

"So, you were one of those kids who used to come over all the time?"

She shook her head. "No, I avoided you like the plague." Her voice was hard. "You were always after little boys. I knew because I was a girl that I was safe, but I didn't want anything to do with you."

His eyes narrowed. "You'd better watch your mouth, young lady."

She snorted. "Why should I? You sent this asshole into my home to torment me … to torment my guests … and for what? What the hell were you expecting?" she scoffed. "You can't use the same tricks you use on little boys with big ones. So you had to be sending a message to them."

"You don't know nothing," Poppy roared. "It was a message. But you don't know what kind. And obviously they are too stupid too."

Geir wished she would choose this time to put the brakes on instead of deciding to be independent and stand up to a gunman. "What message?" Geir asked, trying to calm Poppy down. "That you can get at us anywhere? Anytime?

Considering that we caught your messenger, then I guess the joke's on you."

Geir just needed the right moment to lunge forward. But, as long as that gun was pointed at Morning, he had no chance to grab it. It might go off accidentally, and no way in hell would he get her hurt.

Jager was on the other side of him. They exchanged a hard glance, and suddenly Poppy fired the gun.

Morning cried out in shock.

Ken collapsed over her desk, spreading blood all over her paperwork as it gushed from the bullet hole in his forehead.

But for Jager it was perfect. With that deadly left of his, he coldcocked Poppy right in the throat. With a weird gurgling sound, Poppy fell forward, flat-faced into the carpet.

Geir jumped on him, grabbing the gun from his hand, tossing it to Jager, pulling the old man's hands together to secure them behind his back. He need not worry because Poppy was out cold. And, unfortunately, his face looked to be red, as he struggled to breathe.

Shit," Geir roared. He ripped open the old man's shirt and checked his breathing. "Call for an ambulance," he ordered Jager. "The last thing I want is to have this asshole die before we get answers."

Geir watched his chest rise and fall steadily while they waited for the cops to show up. Poppy was breathing but still unconscious. Geir didn't know if Jager's chop to the throat had done this or if all the excitement had caused a heart attack. By the time the cops got here and the ambulance arrived, Geir was afraid it would be too late. He had mixed emotions about performing CPR on this sick pedophile, but he decided he would, if it came to that.

The sirens could now be heard blocks away.

And suddenly paramedics pushed Geir out of the way.

He stepped off to the side, pulled Morning into his arms and walked her onto the front porch. A car pulled up to the front of the house. Jager had contacted the same detective, who was ready to go into action when they called. He got out of his car and raced toward them.

"It's Poppy," Geir said. "He shot the man he sent here after us. We wrestled the gun away and him to the ground, but he's having a medical emergency of some kind—possibly a heart attack. I don't know if he'll make it. I'll be freaking pissed if he doesn't. We need answers from him."

The detective went inside but was brushed out of the way as the paramedics wheeled Poppy to the ambulance.

Jager came out with the detective. The four watched as the ambulance pulled away. The detective looked at Geir and Jager. "So does bad shit naturally happen around you guys, or are you really talented in that area?"

It was Morning who burst out laughing. "You know? That might be the best question asked tonight." She stood in the circle of Geir's arms. "These guys saved my life, and I won't forget that."

The detective looked down at her and smiled. "Sounds like you've got yourself a couple guardian angels."

She nodded. "And, for that, I'm very grateful."

The detective sighed. "It'll be a long night. Let's get started with your statements."

CHAPTER 15

M ANY HOURS LATER, Morning bustled around the
kitchen, putting on coffee and trying to show some
spirit. She wasn't exactly sure what was happening. She was
afraid the men were leaving, and her heart was already
aching. She thought about everything that had happened
and how her house, her safety net, had been ripped away by
Poppy's activities. She stopped and stared out in the backyard, thinking about the man who had run across it.

It had probably been Ken, and he'd been in the house as
one of her guests. He was the one who had tossed the rooms.
He was the one who had placed the stuffed mouse on her
father's bed. Its sole purpose was a psychological dig into the
minds of Geir and Jager as they sought information regard-
ing their teammate Mouse. She was grateful she knew now,
but, at the same time, it was horrifying to think somebody
could just come into her place and do something like that.

A hand, gentle and warm and huge, landed on her
shoulder. She turned to see Geir looking down at her, a
worried look on his face. She bolstered a smile. "I'm fine,
just lots to think about."

He nodded and tugged her into his arms for a quick
hug. "Hopefully the worst of it's over now."

She nodded, her eyes downcast. She chewed on her bottom lip until he reached out his finger, nudging her chin up.

"What's the matter?"

She took a huge breath. "Are you leaving now?"

He didn't answer for a long moment, just stared into her eyes. "Soon, yes."

She nodded and stepped back, trying to detach herself from the pain she knew was already coming.

"Are you staying here?"

She turned to look at him. "Do you mean, in the house?"

"In the house, in San Diego?"

She shrugged. "I don't know. Everything has happened so fast. Do I want to stay here any longer? No, not now." She brushed her hair out of her eyes. "Am I open to options? Yes. Absolutely, yes."

Just then Jager walked into the kitchen. "That was the detective. Poppy is awake at the hospital and wants to know if we want to meet with him there."

Geir snapped to action. "We so do." He turned to look at her. "Will you be okay if we disappear for a little bit?"

She smiled and nodded. "I'll be fine." She glanced at the clock. "It's eight o'clock. I have to be at the gallery at ten anyway."

He smiled, leaned closer, kissed her hard and said, "I'm sorry I can't accompany you like I had originally planned. But don't worry. You'll be great."

And just like that they were gone. She scrubbed her face, tears already in the corners of her eyes. *She'd be great*, huh? Maybe not so much anymore. But she didn't have time to wallow.

She had to wrap the paintings and get them into the car securely. And that would take some time. Plus, get herself presentable.

She poured herself a cup of coffee and walked up to the studio, happy the worst was over. She hoped Poppy lived, and she hoped he went to prison for the rest of his life. So many lives had been ruined. She couldn't even imagine how Ken got involved in this. What kind of money do you pay to have somebody stay in a bed-and-breakfast and just cause general chaos? She realized Ken was toying with Geir and Jager and likely checking to see what they'd learned about Poppy and Mouse—if anything.

After getting dressed, she headed to her studio. There she opened the French doors, turned on the lights, smiled when she saw the painting she'd completed the night before. She unfolded a table she kept up there and brought out canvas wrapping. Gently she wrapped the four paintings, doing the black one last.

Carefully she carried them one at a time to her car, placing them in the back, the seat folded down so the canvases could lie on top of each other. When they were secured, she went back inside, checked herself in the mirror to make sure she looked okay, which today was white capri pants, a turquoise blouse with three-quarter-length sleeves that flowed and a matching scarf in her hair. She had applied a little bit of makeup, then decided she looked bohemian enough today to be an artist. Besides, after only a few hours' sleep, she could do only so much to hide her lack of sleep. She grabbed her purse and her keys, locked up the house and walked out.

At her car she stopped and took another look at the place she'd called home for a long time. The thing was, it didn't feel like home anymore. Maybe it never would again.

As she sat in her car, she put on her seat belt and slowly backed out of the driveway. She stopped when she saw

Nancy crossing the street to go to Morning's house to look after the place, holding up a big sign that read YOU'LL BE GREAT. GOOD LUCK.

Morning honked her horn and headed to the gallery.

This was such a momentous time for her, along with everything else that had gone on recently. It had helped her set her priorities straight. And she realized how much she wanted to paint, how much she wanted to explore this new part of herself, this new technique, this new bit of creation. She didn't even know how to explain it.

Half an hour later, she pulled into the gallery parking lot and walked inside to see if Leon was there. He was waiting for her.

"Did you bring the paintings?" he asked, his tone brisk.

She took a deep breath and nodded. "I'll get them from the car."

He nodded. "Place whatever you brought on that table." He pointed to it.

With a quick nod again, she walked outside to her car and carefully unloaded the four canvases. When she had them on the table, she stood nervously beside them. They were still wrapped.

He waved at them impatiently. "Open them up."

She unwrapped them, realizing he had set out four easels for her. The paintings could only be seen from one corner in the room. She took a deep breath and carefully placed each one on an easel until everything was presented properly. There was no sign of him.

She waited nervously.

Finally he came out of his office, the look on his face bland, as though he were only going through the motions, like he didn't want to be here. Or rather, didn't want her to be here. He walked around to stand at her side.

He took a look. She heard him catch his breath, noted the way he leaned in, his gaze narrowing as he silently moved from one painting to the next, then back to the first again. His shoulders relaxed, his demeanor changing, and finally he turned to her. "You're very talented."

She'd been holding herself so tensely, but now she wanted to throw her arms around him, hug him. But she didn't dare. She did manage to force out a light breath, and, with an elegant nod, she said, "Thank you."

Inside she couldn't stop smiling.

"ANY IDEA WHAT she'll do with the place?" Jager asked as they walked into the hospital.

"No clue," Geir said. "Hate to see her stay in it all alone though. The nightmares alone could be pretty rough."

Both men nodded. They knew exactly what nightmares entailed and how debilitating they could be. "Do you think she'll move?"

"I don't know," Geir said softly. "It's hardly fair to ask her. This is her home."

"Oh, I think that cocoon has been ripped open already. I think a butterfly is ready to emerge," Jager said. "All butterflies have an instinctive homing ability. You just point her in the direction, and she'll come quite happily."

"Is it fair though?"

"Absolutely it is. She can paint anywhere in the world. And, after this show, if you're right and if her paintings are as good as you say they are, she'll make a hell of a name for herself. New Mexico is big in the arts too. She would no longer be limited to just San Diego."

Geir nodded. "I was thinking the same thing. But I don't want to rush her. I could come back in a week or two, maybe stay with her for a few days, see how we do."

"You could. But I have a suspicion you won't need to."

They walked up to the room they were told Poppy was in to see a policeman standing guard outside. He took one look at them and barked, "Who are you?"

They identified themselves and said Detective Nelson was expecting them.

The cop nodded, opened the door, poked his head in and told the detective, who apparently was inside, that they were here. The policeman nodded, and the two men entered.

Another guard was inside. Poppy was no longer the big robust man he'd been with a gun. The bravado and stuffing was gone. The heart attack had taken much of that away from him. He glared at the men. Even the defiance in his eyes was only half-hearted. Finally he asked, "Why do you care about me after all this time? Isn't it too late to give a damn?"

"We know you shot the young man in one of your houses and Ken in the B&B office. But the dead man found in your house, stabbed weeks or months ago? Plus the dead man in an alley, ... are they both your victims?" Jager asked.

Poppy stared as if trying to remember a couple victims from a pool of possibilities. Then he gave a slight disinterested shrug. "I don't know the victim in the alley, but the lifestyle of those who spend time there is dangerous."

"And the man in your house?" Jager nudged. He shared a glance with Geir.

"What can I say? He wasn't the type of man I thought he was. I didn't plan to kill him, but ... he made me mad."

"Mad?" Geir asked softly. "You buried a knife in his chest."

"He said something ugly about someone I love." His gaze sharpened. "That man was nothing."

There was a moment of silence, then Poppy, coughing slightly, said, "But he's not why you're here. So why?" He leaned back and closed his eyes.

Geir said simply, "Mouse."

Poppy's eyes popped open. He rolled his head to the side and groaned. "That damn kid. God, I loved him. And he loved me."

"What can you tell me about him?" Geir asked.

"Only that I loved him like a son. I loved him like a lover. He was everything to me. And he felt the same way. But he had dreams that didn't include me. Whereas he *was* my dream."

"Why did Mouse leave?"

There was another silence, this one for a long moment.

Geir figured Poppy was trying to figure out how much they knew and how much trouble he was in. "We already know you forged the documents, and he stepped into Ryan Hanson's shoes. But that wasn't the name he was born with, was it?"

Poppy's eyebrows rose. "Interesting ..."

"It's the only way he could become a SEAL, wasn't it?"

"Absolutely. After he left home, he and Lance moved in with me here for a while, until they fell out, and Lance left. But that whole time, the dream of becoming a SEAL was all Mouse would talk about. Who are you guys, and how do you even know he was a SEAL?"

"He was in our unit," Jager said. "What did you do with the man he replaced?"

Poppy winced. "He met with an unfortunate accident. I felt bad about that. But I'd have done anything for Mouse."

"So why place the stuffed mouse in Morning's house?" Geir asked, bewildered. "Mouse is dead. What could you even hope to achieve? And how did you know we were here?"

Poppy looked at him. "You really don't know, do you?"

Geir shook his head. "What is it we don't know?"

At that, Poppy started to laugh. Great big waves of laughter. "Wow. You really don't know. Well, I won't be the one to tell you. You've come this far on your own. You'll have to do the rest of the work yourself." Then he coughed. And he coughed and coughed.

The detective ushered them out into the hall and called for a nurse. The machine went off inside the room, and a crash cart and a medical team came racing.

Geir stared at Poppy. "That's not fair. That's so not fair."

The detective reached out a hand. "Easy. He might survive this. He might not. You know a little more. Maybe that's enough."

Jager's voice was hard. "Hell no, it's not enough. What did he mean, we came this far and can work for the rest?"

Detective Nelson looked at him and said, "Well, maybe you should tell me what he meant about the young man who met his early demise. Are you telling me Poppy murdered somebody?"

"I'm pretty sure you'll find Poppy murdered dozens of people," Geir said quietly. "The two in his house for sure, Ken at Morning's B&B. Also the man whose identity Mouse stole. And we have to consider Poppy might have been involved in the murders of our families and friends—

although why, I don't know. Originally he did everything he could to help Mouse reach his dream. Instead of Mouse going through the training like every other naval officer, Poppy took a shortcut that cost a young man his life and gave us somebody incredibly poorly trained. It explains all the times we had to help Mouse deal with things. We couldn't believe how absolutely inept he was. But it's amazing because we never went on active missions. We trained most of the time, and he was gone a lot of the time. He also broke his leg and was always sick. He spent way too much time out of training. It was a joke how he was not SEAL material, but he was part of us, a part of our unit," Jager added. "So we did everything we could to make him do better."

Geir shook his head and said, "Goddamn it. We're so damn close."

Just then the hospital room door opened, and the doctor stepped out. He looked at the detective and shook his head. Then he turned and walked away.

And Geir realized Poppy had had the last laugh after all.

EPILOGUE

J AGER ELSTAD SHIFTED impatiently. He couldn't wait for the surprise to happen. He'd been instrumental in making it come about, but a bit of doubt remained if he'd done the right thing.

Geir was slumped in Badger's living room. Dotty, as if understanding his mood, lay at his side. Jager knew all his friend thought about was finding a way or an excuse to get back to Morning. She and Geir had talked constantly for the last two weeks, but this long-distance stuff sucked.

Finally Badger said, "Geir, are you with us?"

"I'm here," Geir responded, his voice heavy. "What the hell are we doing now?"

"The same as we always were," Badger said. "So far we ran Poppy down. We confirmed that our Mouse impersonated Ryan Hanson. The police and NCIS are looking into what happened to the original Ryan."

"And yet we still don't know who betrayed us," Jager growled. "That's pissing me right off."

Just then the doorbell rang. Dotty jumped up barking as Kat walked from the living room toward the front door. A muttering of voices was heard there.

Jager looked over to find Geir still staring up at the ceiling. Everybody else knew about the surprise, except for Geir. He'd been like a lovesick teenager since returning from San

Diego, so the unit had finally gone behind Geir's back to make something happen.

Kat walked into the room, and Jager grinned. Beside Kat stood a very hesitant, a very nervous Morning Blossom. Jager looked over at Badger.

Badger studied Morning with interest. Dotty was wiggling at Morning's legs, her tail wagging furiously. Morning had a hand down on the gentle dog's head, but her gaze was on Geir.

Jager hopped up. "Whatever else has to be done, it'll be my mission. You've all had your turn to lead one leg of this. Now it's mine."

Geir shook his head, but he hadn't turned to look toward the front doorway. "It'll be me again. You can't go alone."

"You're not coming with me," Jager said cheerfully, wondering how long it would take Geir to notice his visitor.

"And why the hell not?" Geir lifted his head and glared at him. "No way in hell I'll stay—" His gaze locked on Morning Blossom. He bolted to his feet, raced across the room, caught her up in his arms, twirled her around and crushed her against him.

She burst out laughing, her arms wrapped around him as she hung on tight. Dotty barked several times then, when ignored, wandered back to Badger's side.

Overcome with emotion, Jager had to turn away. He'd helped bring this about, but, at the same time, something made him so very sad. He was the only one alone now. Not that he ever wanted anything like that for himself, but how did he face his six buddies and all their partners and be the odd man out? He shoved his hands into his pockets and said, "I might have to go back to the beginning."

Badger stared at him. "Are you serious? Back to Kabul?"

"Do you have any other suggestions? Any other lines to pull?" Jager asked. "I thought for sure we'd find the answers in California, and we came to a dead end there. That was Mouse's launching point to get into the navy. But we didn't find another lover there. We didn't find another person who would want to go after us because of Mouse's death."

"Should we contact the stepfather again?" Badger asked.

"No," Talon said. "He doesn't know anything. He's been gone from Mouse's life for a long time."

"Well, this is something at least," Erick said, shaking the cell phone in his hand as he walked into the living room from the kitchen. "I just spoke with Nelson, the San Diego detective handling Poppy's file." Erick wore a wide grin, but the gleam in his eyes said a whole lot more. "Their initial investigation so far came up with a name found in some files kept at Poppy's main residence. The detective wanted to know if it meant anything to us or not. Mouse had a good friend, Freddie Brown."

"And where was this good friend?" Badger asked.

"In Colorado."

Talon frowned. "Where in Colorado?"

"Worked in Vail. At one of the big hotels and was a lifty part time."

"Can we call him? Talk to him on the phone?"

"He disappeared a few days ago. Nobody knows where he is." Erick's smile turned predatory. "That's why the detective called us, to track him down. We have a name and a place."

"Damn it," Jager said. Then he froze, and his heart seized. "I'm definitely going. That's where my parents' motorhome ran off the road."

At that moment, Geir returned, carrying Morning Blossom in his arms, his face beaming. He let her down gently on her feet, and she raced across the room and flung her arms around Jager.

He hugged her tight and whispered, "Nice entrance."

She pushed her hair back, beamed up at him and said, "Thank you. For everything."

He dropped a kiss on her forehead. "You look after him. That big bear needs somebody."

She stepped out of Jager's arms, gave him a misty smile and said, "So do you." She patted his cheek. "You're next."

At that, the men burst out laughing. Jager just glared at her. He shook his head and walked to the front door. "If you get more information, let me know."

"Where are you going?" Badger called out.

Jager turned. "Hunting in Vail."

"Brown might not be there anymore."

Jager waved a hand. "Maybe not, but, if he had anything to do with my parents' deaths, I will find him."

This concludes Book 6 of SEALs of Steel: Geir.
Read about Jager: SEALs of Steel, Book 7

SEALS OF STEEL: JAGER BOOK 7

When an eight-man unit hit a landmine, all were injured but one died. The remaining seven aim to see Mouse's death avenged.

On the hunt for answers about who set up the trap, Jager tracks Mouse's friend to Colorado only to discover he's disappeared.

Allison gets caught up in the investigation and the attraction to Jager is undeniable. Passion turns to deadly purpose when they follow a killer to Santa Fe, where he's hunting badgers...

Book 7 is available now!

To find out more visit Dale Mayer's website.

http://smarturl.it/dmjager

Author's Note

Thank you for reading Geir: SEALs of Steel, Book 6! If you enjoyed the book, please take a moment and leave a short review.

Dear reader,

I love to hear from readers, and you can contact me at my website: www.dalemayer.com or at my Facebook author page. To be informed of new releases and special offers, sign up for my newsletter or follow me on BookBub. And if you are interested in joining Dale Mayer's Fan Club, here is the Facebook sign up page.
facebook.com/groups/402384989872660

Cheers,
Dale Mayer

Your Free Book Awaits!

KILL OR BE KILLED

Part of an elite SEAL team, Mason takes on the dangerous jobs no one else wants to do – or can do. When he's on a mission, he's focused and dedicated. When he's not, he plays as hard as he fights.

Until he meets a woman he can't have but can't forget. Software developer, Tesla lost her brother in combat and has no intention of getting close to someone else in the military. Determined to save other US soldiers from a similar fate, she's created a program that could save lives. But other countries know about the program, and they won't stop until they get it – and get her.

Time is running out ... For her ... For him ... For them ...

DOWNLOAD a *complimentary* copy of MASON? Just tell me where to send it!

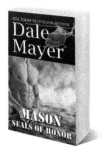

http://dalemayer.com/sealsmason/

About the Author

Dale Mayer is a USA Today bestselling author best known for her Psychic Visions and Family Blood Ties series. Her contemporary romances are raw and full of passion and emotion (Second Chances, SKIN), her thrillers will keep you guessing (By Death series), and her romantic comedies will keep you giggling (It's a Dog's Life and Charmin Marvin Romantic Comedy series).

She honors the stories that come to her – and some of them are crazy and break all the rules and cross multiple genres!

To go with her fiction, she also writes nonfiction in many different fields with books available on resume writing, companion gardening and the US mortgage system. She has recently published her Career Essentials Series. All her books are available in print and ebook format.

Connect with Dale Mayer Online

Dale's Website – www.dalemayer.com
Twitter – @DaleMayer
Facebook – facebook.com/DaleMayer.author
BookBub – bookbub.com/authors/dale-mayer

Also by Dale Mayer

Published Adult Books:

Psychic Vision Series
Tuesday's Child
Hide 'n Go Seek
Maddy's Floor
Garden of Sorrow
Knock Knock...
Rare Find
Eyes to the Soul
Now You See Her
Shattered
Into the Abyss
Seeds of Malice
Eye of the Falcon
Itsy-Bitsy Spider
Psychic Visions Books 1–3
Psychic Visions Books 4–6
Psychic Visions Books 7–9

By Death Series
Touched by Death
Haunted by Death
Chilled by Death
By Death Books 1–3

Charmin Marvin Romantic Comedy Series

Broken Protocols
Broken Protocols 2
Broken Protocols 3
Broken Protocols 3.5
Broken Protocols 1-3

Broken and... Mending

Skin
Scars
Scales (of Justice)
Broken but... Mending 1-3

Glory

Genesis
Tori
Celeste
Glory Trilogy

Biker Blues

Morgan: Biker Blues, Volume 1
Cash: Biker Blues, Volume 2

SEALs of Honor

Mason: SEALs of Honor, Book 1
Hawk: SEALs of Honor, Book 2
Dane: SEALs of Honor, Book 3
Swede: SEALs of Honor, Book 4
Shadow: SEALs of Honor, Book 5
Cooper: SEALs of Honor, Book 6
Markus: SEALs of Honor, Book 7
Evan: SEALs of Honor, Book 8

Mason's Wish: SEALs of Honor, Book 9

Chase: SEALs of Honor, Book 10

Brett: SEALs of Honor, Book 11

Devlin: SEALs of Honor, Book 12

Easton: SEALs of Honor, Book 13

Ryder: SEALs of Honor, Book 14

Macklin: SEALs of Honor, Book 15

Corey: SEALs of Honor, Book 16

Warrick: SEALs of Honor, Book 17

SEALs of Honor, Books 1–3

SEALs of Honor, Books 4–6

SEALs of Honor, Books 7–10

SEALs of Honor, Books 11–13

Heroes for Hire

Levi's Legend: Heroes for Hire, Book 1

Stone's Surrender: Heroes for Hire, Book 2

Merk's Mistake: Heroes for Hire, Book 3

Rhodes's Reward: Heroes for Hire, Book 4

Flynn's Firecracker: Heroes for Hire, Book 5

Logan's Light: Heroes for Hire, Book 6

Harrison's Heart: Heroes for Hire, Book 7

Saul's Sweetheart: Heroes for Hire, Book 8

Dakota's Delight: Heroes for Hire, Book 9

Tyson's Treasure: Heroes for Hire, Book 10

Jace's Jewel: Heroes for Hire, Book 11

Rory's Rose: Heroes for Hire, Book 12

Brandon's Bliss: Heroes for Hire, Book 13

Liam's Lily: Heroes for Hire, Book 14

North's Nikki: Heroes for Hire, Book 15

Heroes for Hire, Books 1–3

Heroes for Hire, Books 4–6

Heroes for Hire, Books 7–9

SEALs of Steel
Badger: SEALs of Steel, Book 1
Erick: SEALs of Steel, Book 2
Cade: SEALs of Steel, Book 3
Talon: SEALs of Steel, Book 4
Laszlo: SEALs of Steel, Book 5
Geir: SEALs of Steel, Book 6
Jager: SEALs of Steel, Book 7
The Last Wish: SEALs of Steel, Book 8

Collections
Dare to Be You...
Dare to Love...
Dare to be Strong...
RomanceX3

Standalone Novellas
It's a Dog's Life
Riana's Revenge
Second Chances

Published Young Adult Books:

Family Blood Ties Series
Vampire in Denial
Vampire in Distress
Vampire in Design
Vampire in Deceit
Vampire in Defiance
Vampire in Conflict